THE PRISONER

Sara Thomson

First Published 2020

This edition published in 2020 by Home Front Books

For further information on the author, permission requests or any other aspect of this work visit https://sarathomsonauthor.co.uk

ISBN:
ISBN-978-1-9999636-1-3

Happy reading!
Sara Thomson

For my first childhood friend -
someone who showed me there were kind and selfless people in a world of childhood darkness, and who was never able to be free from darkness herself.
This is for you.

CHAPTER ONE

November 1940 Anna

Anna subconsciously pulled the blanket tighter around herself as another thud shook the building, closer this time. She brushed the shower of brick dust from her lap and sipped her hot cocoa, if only for something to do with her hands.

Olivia frowned as she glanced towards the basement ceiling, a slight worry line creasing her perfect brow. Then equally as quickly, it was gone and she continued, her voice not betraying whatever it was she'd been thinking.

"I got my first letter today."

"From who?" Anna asked.

"Lieutenant Mickey Johnson. You remember the airman I was stepping out with who disappeared on a mission."

Anna nodded confirmation, but in truth she only half remembered the tall airman on the few occasions she'd seen him, passing in the hallway as one or the other of them was entering or leaving.

Olivia continued, "Well it seems he's okay and in a POW camp in Germany."

"Oh goodness, really?"

Olivia nodded. "I'll read you his letter."

"You don't have to do that." Anna waved her hand for Olivia to put it away and took a swallow of the hot liquid.

"Of course I do darling, who else am I going to share it with?"

She fished out the letter from her dressing gown pocket as another thud shook the walls. Anna glanced up again, before turning her attention back to Olivia, who was now smoothing out the neatly written letter already showed the signs of dog-eared corners.

"Dear Olivia,

I hope you are well and not too busy with your nursing work to find time to read this. I'm happy to report I'm fit and well and safely ensconced in a camp in Germany with a number of other RAF officers. We're a small bunch but growing all the time, more's the pity. The weather here is bitterly cold, dry and sharp - it's like icicles when you breathe.

On the whole things aren't too bad although roll call each day is rather dreary. I do hope you will write back, I'm desperate for news of home, so all the boys rely on our womenfolk to write and tell us how things are fairing over there, the news we get is very sketchy.

Food here isn't great, and I must say the Germans eat some unusual dishes, but I'm surviving. Many of the boys entertain themselves by teaching each other. We have a language learning group, a football team, a bridge club and a great many other things to keep busy with.

However, it's not all a picnic in the park, we are not allowed to forget we are prisoners.

The guards told us the war is over for us now and somehow it doesn't seem real when everyone else is still fighting and we are sat here entertaining ourselves with cards and lessons.

Anyway, do write back and tell me news of you and how things are at home. I miss it all dreadfully.

Best wishes

Lt Johnson.

"Best wishes?" Anna said. "That's odd."

"Odd how?"

"Well, you'd been stepping out with him for a few weeks and he says best wishes?"

Anything Olivia might have said in reply was drowned out by a thud so loud the whole cellar and ground above vibrated around them. Some of the other girls screamed and one started to cry. Sounds of glass breaking and furniture falling was all mixed up in one giant din.

Anna and Olivia crouched further into the corner in an attempt to make themselves as small as possible. Anna glanced at Olivia. She was staring up at the basement ceiling, her lips white.

Anna wondered what she was thinking about and reached for her hand. Olivia clung on tightly and they eventually dozed off like that for a few hours.

As the dawn light rose slowly, Anna rushed down the steps of her boarding house. The all clear had only sounded a little while ago and she'd been awake most of the night. She was a little surprised the street hadn't been flattened by the bomb that landed very close by, but apart from a few broken windows, her boarding house had miraculously escaped lasting damage this time. Olivia was long gone, off to the hospital for her shift and had been twitchy and restless all night, even after the all clear. Anna wondered if she'd been thinking about the casualties she'd been busy with and had noticed Olivia seemed a little quieter and more withdrawn than usual. Anna glanced up at the dark stormy November sky, pulling her coat around her more tightly. A sharp bitter twinge in the crisp morning air made Anna's sleep-deprived brain startle, giving her some much needed morning clarity.

A shout behind made her turn and look. The postman was flapping a little square envelope at her and hurrying along in a lopsided manner. She stopped, allowing him to catch up. He panted beside her, his woollen scarf loosening a little as he hoisted his bag higher, and briefly mopped his brow before handing her the envelope.

"Morning' Miss Forrester. I thought it was you. Only one today Miss." He tapped his hat and continued his rounds.

Anna stared down at the rough envelope beneath her fingertips, the thick paper almost foreign and distasteful. Familiar handwriting was scrawled across it like a squashed black insect smeared along its width. Her heart shuddered sending a wave of dread through her body. It was him. She knew without opening it. Just as she knew what the letter would say. Damn him. Why couldn't he just leave it alone?

She shoved the little letter roughly into her bag not caring whether it got crumpled, shut the clasp a little more forcibly than necessary and continued on her way determinedly, shoving unwelcome thoughts about Doctor Laker from her mind, her feet tap-tapping along the pavement.

Damn him!

Ahead, more houses had windows blown out. As she gingerly picked her way over glass fragments and bits of rubble crunching and cracking under her feet, she couldn't help but wonder whether they would always be this lucky, but closed down the thought before it had time to develop into something more sinister. She would not dwell on such things.

Some of the residents at this end of the street had begun to emerge in the dusty morning light. Most gave her a smile and a nod; the reflected look of relief that everything was all right for another day mirrored on every face.

An elderly man was calmly sweeping glass from the front of his little step, and nodded at Anna as she passed, a strong smell of pipe tobacco mixed with dust drifting from him.

Passing the top of her road and moving towards the bomb

site, she could see, even from this distance, that the affected street, a few rows down, had suffered considerable damage. Her imagination relayed imaginary scenes of people trapped, injured and dying beneath rubble, its weight pressing down on their bodies so they couldn't breathe, limbs unable to move. Her eyes felt hot and she blinked away the thoughts. Lately her emotions seemed to always be simmering below the surface, threatening to spill over. An image of her mother passed behind her eyes and she pushed it away determined not to let grief control her.

A policeman at the top of the bombed-out street was discussing something with a bushy, grey mustachioed man in a suit and a couple of young boys were looking longingly down what was left of the cordoned-off street. She knew children still left in the city collected aeroplane salvage and getting a prize item piece of Luftwaffe plane, or shrapnel, was treasured above all.

As she passed the small band, she heard the policeman say in a thick east-end accent, "Now I'm watching you boys. Don't go down that street."

She didn't look at the boys faces but heard them sigh audibly with all the disappointment of childhood and smiled at the innocence.

Several of the houses in the damaged street had been blasted into pieces. Piles of broken bricks, sections of roof, glass and debris blocked the road in a huge pile of destruction. Clouds of dust hovered above the mess and faint smoke trails spiralled upwards in long streams.

A workman was examining a section of precarious looking wall further down the street and she could just make out a fireman on top of a ladder, at the other side of the chaos. The acrid smell of dust, plaster, damp and soot invaded her airways and made her cough.

Memories of the book shop raid crept into her mind;

deafening thuds pounding all night; fear of death; the morning after; the house blown to bits; body parts strewn across the street; a disconnected arm with the engagement ring still on one finger.

She continued on forcing herself to concentrate on her own footsteps.

Her mind stubbornly returned to the turmoil that had started with the death of her mother, and led to the truth, not only about her mother's life, but her own. She couldn't help wishing things had been different; her mother had been able to talk to her. A strong sense of loss followed her, like a stray dog, no matter how she tried to ignore it, and the reality that she could do nothing to change things did nothing to suppress her anger at the whole situation and the lack of control she felt.

Her thoughts were momentarily interrupted when she almost ran into a man in a brown suit, his hat pulled down low over his face, head bent.

"I'm sorry," she said startled.

Instead of a reply he grunted at her and hurried in the other direction. She watched him for a moment, and he glanced back at her before hurrying away faster.

What a rude man, she thought and continued her journey, swapping her bag from one arm to the other.

Then there was Doctor Laker, his face swam into her thoughts and her mind strayed to the unopened letter. She became conscious of the firm leather handles of her bag beneath her grip, the weight of that letter making it feel heavier. She sighed. If she was truly honest she didn't know what to say to him. This right now, going to Fleet Street through broken, bombed streets, finding news and spending nights on hard, dirty cellar floors, was all she wanted. She didn't expect him to understand and she wasn't prepared to explain herself. Things would be fine if she could forget the whole thing and go back to work as normal. Anna swapped her bag to the other arm again, determined not to think of the doctor. She had already made up her mind not to read his latest letter. She was bloody well certain she didn't want to know what it said.

He just needed to realise they had no future. She still hated the irritating, annoying man he was every bit as much as she always had and still thought romance bloody silly. Did he not say in the beginning he had hated her? Did they not fight constantly?

Then the kiss came into her thoughts; his hands gently caressing her face. He had taken advantage of her moment of weakness, due to the shock of being mugged and injured. She blinked the thoughts away forcibly, as she moved down the dirty, stone steps towards the tube station. He was not important.

Old men in suits and hats, women in various uniforms and a mother with her children sat opposite her on the tube as it whooshed and rattled along towards the city. The smell of dust and damp followed them down from the destruction on the streets above. Anna noticed the looks of disapproval at the children still in the city. She thought of that street this morning and the stories the girls were telling last night and then again, glanced at the mother, the woman's face set in defiance, her chin jutting out in defence. She knew what everyone was saying about her.

The family only served to remind Anna that her own had been nothing but a lie built on hidden secrets for generations, and the fact that her mother turned out to be a Lady, not just any, a bloody Leyac, one of the most well known names in the country, didn't make the situation any easier, but despite everything, she still wished more than anything to have her mother back.

As the tube shushed to a stop Anna stood leaving the mother, her children and the other passengers and stepping onto the platform, glancing backwards, she felt the wind of the train's departure blow her dress as she watched it disappear into the dark tunnel.

When she reached her Fleet Street office, she was still thinking of the children on the tube and barely remembered the walk from the station. The newspaper office was busy with people but they all stopped and looked up as she entered. She gave them a weak smile, her neck prickling as she felt eyes watching her. She turned her back to the room but could still feel their eyes watching every move she made. Alarm made her heart pound and she took a few deep breaths. She stared up through the grimy window and the grey clouds drifting by as she purposely removed her coat, hat and scarf.

"Forrester!" Her editor's bark had a note of annoyance that made Anna jump and her heart sank to her stomach.

What now?

She turned to see him motion from the doorway with his thumb for her to get in his office. Sighing, she flung her coat casually across the chair and felt the eyes move to the editor's office with her.

She closed the door as he sat back in his chair, the familiar woodbine clamped between his teeth, smoke puffing around him in a fog.

"Sit," he said taking the cigarette and stubbing it out furiously.

"Sir, have I done something wrong?"

He laughed then. "She asks me if she's done something wrong."

He picked up the paper on his desk and threw it at her

with force. She caught it, giving him a questioning look.

He opened his pack of woodbines and lit another cigarette, shaking the match out. "Have you read today's paper Forrester?"

"No, I..." She opened out the paper and looked at the front page. In that moment the headline; words printed in stark harsh type stared back at her, taunting. Her whole body surged with cold dread and she sat frozen in the moment, the crisp paper rough and harsh in her hands. She blinked hoping that the words would change, but no. She had only ever experienced such shock at one other moment in her life; the day she had discovered the secret that her mother was a lady thought dead since 1915, hidden away under a new identity. The confusion and anger of that moment came rushing back, mixed together in a cocktail of disquiet.

She read and reread the title.

LEYAC TWIN FOUND

She didn't need to read the article. She didn't want to; couldn't.

She looked up at him now anger fighting to take over. He squinted at her through his smoke clouds.

"I can see, Forrester, this is a shock." He paused and took another drag on his woodbine. "Now, what I'm annoyed about is that a journalist under my roof, one of my own reporters sat on a story as big as this. And, that it took another reporter to break that story, when she, could have come to me herself. So, tell me Forrester, why did you try to bury one of the biggest non-war stories in the last twenty-five years?"

"Sir, this is my personal life. I made that decision and I stand by it. Whoever wrote this has done so without my knowledge or permission, and frankly I thoroughly dislike being made into the feature of the day." She slammed the paper down on his desk and stood up. "Do you realise the difficult position you have put me in? I agreed with the Leyac estate to keep the truth that I am the missing Leyac twin quiet and this makes it look like I have broken that agreement. I can't tell you how damn annoyed I am at being used in this way."

He remained motionless, looking up at her through shrewd eyes. "I'm not interested in personal ramifications. I'm here to sell papers. You sat on one of the biggest non-war stories we've had for ages and what I'm questioning is whether I can allow you to continue as a reporter for this paper. I can't have my journalists sitting on stories, no matter what."

"Sir, you have to understand the reason this was kept secret was because of a request from the estate themselves. They had been complicit in keeping my mother's identity a secret. They knew she was the mother of the Leyac twins, not, as widely reported, her sister Louisa, and that the missing twin was in fact a girl. It was the Leyac family who essentially concocted the whole thing. It was them who wanted the secret to remain hidden and by writing this damn article you have put me in a difficult position with very dangerous people. All I want is to continue my life the way it was. I've lost my mother and gained a whole host of trouble and unwanted attention. I didn't disclose the story because it's not a story, it's my life."

"I'm just damn irritated that the bloody missing twin everyone's been harping on about for years was right under my nose and I didn't know. What sort of reporter does that make me? I look like a bloody fool. It's only lucky Marcus brought the story to us before any of the competition got wind of it."

"Marcus?" Anna paused as anger surged, " The bloody bastard."

"Forrester. I will not have language like that from a

woman."

"Sir, he helped me solve the mystery, he was there though the whole journey, he knows how dangerous Flynn is. He was there when I made that agreement. He promised to keep the secret."

"Forrester, you fool, he's a reporter. And reporters will report news. You surely didn't expect him to keep it. And it's a bloody good thing too."

Anna flung open the door of the office letting it swing and vibrate on its hinges and marched out.

CHAPTER TWO

Anna

Forrester, get back here. I'm not finished with you." The annoyance was clear in her editor's voice.

She ignored him. She was damn sick of people determining her life - Flynn; the Leyacs; this bloody war; the doctor; her editor, and now bloody Marcus. It was enough. Her face set, she yanked open the door to Marcus' office without knocking and slammed both hands on his desk leaning over him.

Amused and unconcerned he leaned back in his chair and lit a cigarette, took a long drag and blew it out slowly before saying.

"Hello Forrester, thought I might see you today."

"You bastard, you betrayed me."

"I did no such thing, and I don't think language like that is appropriate."

"Never bloody mind the language. How could you?"

"Forrester. I don't see what the issue is. It's a big story."

"You made a promise."

"I did no such thing. You made that deal with Flynn. I made no promise to anyone at all. You, my dear, made the mistake of assuming, and an assumption is worth nothing."

"I thought you were my friend."

"And, you mistook a journalist's nose for a story, for friendship. That is why, Forrester, you will never make it as a reporter. It's not personal. You said yourself in the beginning, breaking something this big would make us. And that is exactly what it has done. I've just got off the phone from a whole host of newspapers offering me jobs. I did exactly what I set out to do. I broke a story. That was all it ever was, a story."

He stubbed out his cigarette and leaned forward towards her.

"Did you really think I'd take time from my job to chase around the country if I didn't think I could break something big?"

"But then we found out that story was me. It changed things."

"Only for you. A story is a story, no matter who it's about. It made no difference to me. My first loyalty is to my career. I don't have loyalty to anything else."

"How can you be so heartless? You know what Flynn did to keep me quiet. He's dangerous. Do you realise what he might do now?"

"You handled him before. I'm sure you can do it now. Forrester, this is of no concern to me. It was simply another story. That's it. There was never anything personal in it. If you were a *real* reporter you would never have lost sight of that."

"Marcus, you can dress it up however you wish, the truth is you betrayed me and you know it." Anna began pacing the little office.

"Wrong Forrester. You betrayed yourself as a journalist. You harp on that I promised to keep it a secret and I betrayed you. But what you're really saying is you're fine breaking stories so long as they aren't about you. When things change and you become the story, you don't like it. Be realistic Forrester. Life doesn't work like that."

Anna suddenly felt tired, a sharp pain in her temple.

"Damn you Marcus."

Her eyes felt hot again and she blinked away threatening emotion. She wasn't about to show him any weakness, so turned to leave.

"What will you do now?" he called after her.

"You really think I will ever tell you anything again?"

"So there's no chance of an interview then?"

She ignored this and walked out leaving him there, a well of sickness and fear knotted in her stomach. Everyone knew; the whole country knew everything.

Her mother's face swam behind her eyes. Mama what have you left me with?

Anna returned to her Editor's office. An air of calm had descended and he was slowly smoking another woodbine, while looking over a stack of papers littering his desk.

He glanced up as she entered, leaning back in his chair watching her.

"What did he say for himself?"

When she didn't respond he continued,

"You shouldn't be hard on him Forrester, he's a good journalist and you could learn a lot."

"That may be so, but he knew I didn't want the story released. It is a betrayal no matter how you view it."

"Well, you are a woman, and I suppose I should expect you to react like a woman, although I do think you're being over the top about it. But as you are a girl and still have a lot to learn, I am prepared to overlook you hiding the story, this time. But, if anything at all happens like this again, I will have to get rid of you."

Anna nodded compliance, despite the anger churning at

the pit of her stomach and the sharp fear that all this could end her career, now mixed with the injustice of her situation. She turned to leave in silence, internally damning the Leyacs and her mother.

"Oh, one more thing Forrester."

She turned and looked at him, her hand gripping the door handle, knuckles turning white.

"What are you going to do about the Leyacs?"

"In what sense?"

"The house, the money... You're the heiress now your twin is dead."

"I don't want any of it. I'll probably just sign it over to the trustee."

"Flynn?"

"Yes that's him."

He raised an eyebrow and nodded taking a long drag on his woodbine.

"I've got a story for you," he said as he blew out smoke through squinted eyes.

"It's a nice easy piece on some new product that's going to help transform the lives of housewives. Some American is doing a presentation on it this afternoon. Go along, see if it's any good and write me a review for the women's column. Here."

He waved a slightly crumpled sheet at her with details of the person she was to see, and the location.

She took the sheet and studied the scrawled handwriting as she left his office.

For once, she was pleased to be given an easy assignment; at least it would take her mind off the mess her life was in. Her job was the one constant left and she was determined to cling to that small sense of normality.

But the doctor's face kept appearing behind her eyes. What would he say to Marcus when he found out? She pushed thoughts of him away. It was none of his business.

Anna put on her coat roughly as she left the office craving a sense of escape. She couldn't wait to get away. For the first time, her office wasn't the haven she was used to.

As she descended the stairs gripping the wooden rail, thoughts of her mother, and what she would have thought of this whole mess, were not far from her mind. At one time she would have been sure she knew what her mother's reaction would have been, but since discovering her mother's secrets she wondered whether she had actually ever known her at all and this thought saddened her.

That sense of sadness, that melancholy that had always sat behind her eyes, that airy false cheerfulness, the almost insistence that Anna believe she had a father, was due to an entirely different reason to that which Anna had always presumed.

Anna's assumption that she had been a bastard had been logical given the facts. Anyone would have thought the same, she told herself, as she negotiated a large crowd of men in matching business suits, animatedly talking amongst themselves, not noticing her. She sidestepped.

Her mother's sadness was because of Harry, the seaman, her father, who her mother had loved dearly according to the diary. The damn diary had sparked off the whole investigation and caused this mess, but in another way she understood her mother so much more now.

She couldn't help but feel a deep sense of sadness when she thought of what she had believed was her mother's fragile, delicate nature, had only been small cracks in a whole depth of hurt and sorrow that she had carried like armour, and no wonder with such a family as she had. The bloody Leyacs'. But they were all dead now, even her twin.

As she waited to cross a busy street, she put her mother to

the back of her mind. The knowledge that she'd never really know the woman who had brought her up left a knot of despair in her stomach.

Her mind swirled with a mixture of emotions and thoughts. She needed to think clearly about how to handle things now her identity was no longer a secret and how the hell was she going to convince Flynn she hadn't broken their deal?

Ten minutes later she had found a little back street cafe with dirty old tables, wobbly chairs and smelt distinctly of greasy fat. The tea was weak and watery but it was hot and she let the steam from the cup settle on her face as she held it to her lips, letting the warmth mixed with the faint smell of hot liquid float across her face.

As she drank the sensation of heat slid down her throat and warmed her inside. All she could see was Flynn's face. What the hell was she going to do? Damn you Anthony Marcus for doing this to me.

She hoped Flynn would be easily convinced and she could simply fade into the background, God knows she didn't want anything to do with that damn house. She thought then of her twin. It was strange to think that she had had a twin, but somehow it wasn't strange at all. She had always felt as if something was missing and had assumed it was her absent father, but maybe it had been someone else all along.

She put her cup down in its mismatched saucer and poured herself more tea from the pot with the chipped lid. As she removed the tea leaf strainer and began to stir her cup, she noticed it had begun to rain again. Soon it would be the beginning of another year she thought as she watched the raindrops splash and bounce. Anna couldn't consider the future; everything was such a mess.

A clattering of pots behind her made her jump and she pulled out the scrap of paper with the directions to the event she was covering. The product they were showcasing was made by an American company. Well she should certainly get plenty to write about.

The door to the cafe clattered open and a couple came in. The girl had fluffy blond hair styled elaborately under her hat; the man, younger, in shirt sleeves looked like he'd come from a factory of some sort. He shifted from foot to foot uncomfortably while she waltzed in with an air of authority. They sat at the opposite side of the cafe, allowing Anna to discreetly observe the pair. The young man ordered tea and the girl coffee. The waitress flounced away and the girl talked a little louder than is discreet in such a small place.

"Well, I can't believe it. Our Tommy says it's a hoax, some fool after the house. What do you reckon?"

The young man shrugs at her question a bored look on his face.

"Oh, you are a bore, come on, what kind of brother are you if you aren't going to join my conversation?"

"Lucy, I don't much care for gossip."

"It 'aint gossip if it's in the paper," the girl said losing some of her put-on accent and reverting to a more natural sounding east-end twang.

The young man laughed and leaned back as the waitress returned with cups, saucers and a teapot.

"Lucy, who really cares?"

"Everyone, it's been one of those unsolved cases for years and now they've found her. Well I'd like to meet this, what's her name, Felix? Farnborough? Give me that paper, let me see." The girl straightened the paper and thumbed to the page she wanted while continuing to talk. "I'd like to meet her and ask her what she's been playin' at all these years. Why didn't she come forward before. Why did she let that poor boy die never knowing, and all them years he searched. It's cruel if you ask me... Ah! Here it is, her name, Anna

Forrester."

The words, like a sting, made Anna jump violently and she dropped her cup spilling tea on the table. Noticing the sudden movement, the girl looked at Anna indifferently, but her expression changed when she looked down at the paper, then back at Anna.

"Hey," she pointed. "That's her there. Look there's a picture right here."

She tapped the paper with her finger staring at Anna, who attempted to gather her things, her hands shaking. How the hell had the girl recognised her? Anna dropped her bag and bent over to retrieve it. As she stood again the girl was behind her.

"You? Where have you been all this time? Are you really the twin or are you after the money? Why didn't you tell your poor brother before he went to war and got killed? And him looking all them years too."

The girl was now barring her way, and Anna had to shove past her to get away, the girl continuing her relentless questions as Anna ran into the rain soaked streets, water splashing her stockings as she ran.

Once she was a fair distance away, she paused to catch her breath, her lungs gasping, her feet sore. Damn it, damn it! She would have to take care of this problem, quickly, so she could move on.

Composing herself, as she passed a somewhat familiar man in a brown suit, his hat pulled down over his face, she focused her attention on her assignment. She was early but decided to go and get a head start.

CHAPTER THREE

Prisoner

Secrets had become a necessary part of his existence and nowhere more so than here. He was all too aware he needed to be careful. The slightest slip-up could get him in solitary or worse.

As it stood, he had little choice, honesty could get him killed, it didn't stop the guilt at his betrayal but some things were more important. He shook his head to disperse the thoughts. He needed to stay alert, it was vital he kept the secret; if they found out, the situation would be much worse for him here.

He sat smoking the last of his red cross cigarettes, he'd bought off Spiffy for his share of yesterday's rations, contemplating what to do about the situation. He wiggled his toes and watched the foot of his shoe move slightly as the toes inside jiggled, absently looking but not really seeing.

He crossed his legs and leaned back on the top of his three-high wooden bunk, blowing smoke slowly at the cracked ceiling.

The door to his hut was flung open and a large imposing shadow in angry stance blocked the doorway, the sunlight behind the figure hiding his face.

"You," the shadow said, "the Kommandant wishes to see you."

The Prisoner took another drag of his cigarette and watched the soldier in the doorway. He lazily blew smoke out before beginning to move. I'll go because I have to but in my own flamin' time, he thought quickly hiding his alarm at being summoned.

"Hurry up," the soldier said stamping his feet.

The prisoner hopped down from his bunk, his boots thudding on the floor, a sound that seemed almost final in its dull echo.

As he got closer to the shadow in the doorway and the winter lights shifted, he could see the face more clearly. He was hardly a man, this figure. Instead, what the prisoner had thought of as imposing, was in fact little more than a boy close-up. A baby-faced profile stared up at him, desperately trying to look important, but the boy had not yet gained the ability to hide his feelings and, despite his best efforts, showed a great deal of false bravado.

The face had big, blue eyes and long eyelashes, and the fluff on his chin showed the promise of stubble yet to appear. The jawline was one that, in a year or so, would not look out of place on a Hollywood film set.

The prisoner felt sorry for the boy, thrust as he was into this war. He was further surprised when he realised that although a boy, he was probably not more than five or six years younger than himself. But the prisoner had seen and done so much in the last few months, he felt the age gap was double that.

The boy stood aside slightly, so the prisoner could step out into the daylight, the cool winter sun shining through the clouds and making him squint as his eyes adjusted from the gloom of his hut. The crisp, cold European air so different from the damp, coldness of home.

The gravel crunched underfoot as they walked down the snaking paths between the rows of huts.

Other prisoners stopped and stared as he went by, a questioning look on their faces. One nudged another stood next to him and whispered something, keeping his eyes fixed on the prisoner.

The prisoner shrugged, a disinterested silent response to their questioning glances, to say he wasn't worried.

This seemed to be acceptable and the other prisoners went back to their conversations, but the prisoner noticed, they each kept one eye on him and watched where he was going.

The boy behind him was taking two steps to his one and was slightly out of breath.

The prisoner looked back at the determined young face, a sense of defiance on the young features. The prisoner smiled, he was just a green boy, probably getting his face wiped by his mother only last month.

They got to the Kommandant's office and the boy called "Actung!" for him to halt and stand to attention.

The prisoner's own sense of defiance crept into his response as the heckles on the back of his neck stood up at the boy's words. He was damn sure he wasn't going to stand to attention under a German order.

Although, he did stop, but lazily with his hands in his pockets.

The boy marched round to face him, his young features spotted with red blotches of anger, "Actung!" he shouted again.

The prisoner gave him an innocent look, "I'm dreadfully sorry, I seem to have forgotten how."

The boy opened his mouth to speak, then thought better of it and instead turned around and marched up to the door to the Kommandant's office, banging on it rather more loudly than necessary.

A muffled voice from inside responded and the boy opened the door, standing to attention in an almost comically stiff way.

The prisoner spoke excellent German, which he hadn't let them know - another necessary secret - so understood the conversation between the Kommandant and the boy. However, feigning ignorance, the prisoner stood at the foot of the stairs and listened.

The Kommandant told the boy he didn't need to bang down his door, he could just knock ordinarily, and that he was grateful for the respect of standing to attention, but it wasn't really necessary every time he came to the office.

The boy told the Kommandant he had brought the prisoner as requested. The Kommandant thanked the boy and told him he could leave.

"Come in," the Kommandant called outside and the boy moved from the doorway. "Close the door," he again commanded as the prisoner entered.

He turned to close the door, the boy had hesitated at the foot of the steps and was watching him, the prisoner raised one eyebrow at the boy and took a small amount of satisfaction in closing the door on him.

He turned to the Kommandant, who was sat behind a big oak desk. Papers were scattered all over it, a half-drunk cup of dark liquid that looked like coffee was steaming beside him and an abandoned cigarette was wafting a stream of smoke into the air in a line to the ceiling.

The Kommandant leaned back in his chair. He was an older man, the prisoner guessed him to be middle fifties. He had a good covering of flesh as someone who had always eaten well, and had suffered from weight gain in later years because of it. Big sandy eyebrows covered quick intelligent eyes and he gave off a pleasant, calm air.

The prisoner had only met him once before but was surprised that someone so personable and relaxed could be placed in charge of a camp like this one. However, the prisoner recognised that his view of German soldiers was coloured by what he had been told, and it had been a shock at first to realise that many were just the same as he.

It had been easier to fight the enemy when he had thought of them as evil monsters, but to actually spend time around these people made him realise they were just the same, fighting a war that neither of them wanted.

"You may sit," the Kommandant said.

The prisoner sat, leaning back against the chair.

"Do you smoke?" the Kommandant asked already opening his packet and lighting two fresh cigarettes, the abandoned one in the ashtray apparently forgotten.

The prisoner took the cigarette and leaned back against the chair once more, squinting at the Kommandant who was watching him, the tension of expectation prickling his skin. This niceness wasn't just for the sake of being pleasant, he was certain of that.

"I have a question for you, Lieutenant…"

Here it comes, he wants something, but what? He again thought of his carefully guarded secrets, so continued the outwardly laid back comfortable position while inside his body was stiff and taught with anticipation and the fear of expectation.

"When you were captured, your plane had been shot down, your colleague was killed but you were not."

"As you can see, Kommandant, I appear to be alive still."

The Kommandant smiled an amused expression. "This troubles me Lieutenant."

"Why is that Kommandant?" The prisoner kept his even, almost mocking tone, but his insides lurched. What does he know?

"I am no expert on aircraft, but it has been suggested that you are not telling the entire truth about what happened."

"Who has suggested such a thing? That's preposterous."

"That is of no consequence, but let us just look at the facts once more Lieutenant."

"Really this is becoming rather tedious."

"Lieutenant, you do not seem to realise the precariousness of your situation."

"On the contrary, I realise implicitly that I'm a prisoner here."

"No Lieutenant, there are some who wish to remove you from this camp and hand you over to other groups for interrogation. So far, I have been able to ensure that you remain here. However, this may not always be the case, if you do not co-operate with my questions." The Kommandant stood and began pacing the room as if giving a lecture.

The prisoner sighed, "We were flying for home. We were shot at. The plane went down, rather badly, the landing was horrendous. Captain was killed and I was injured, I was awoken by a farmer with a pitch fork rammed at me and jabbering in German. Soldiers came, they brought me here. That's about the sum of it."

"You see Lieutenant, that is where the problem lies, because the farmer says he saw you moving around inside the aircraft and when he got closer says it was then you were unconscious. Tell me, how can you be awake one moment then unconscious the next when nothing further has happened to warrant this change?"

"I really can't say, the farmer must have been mistaken, I was most definitely not awake and it's a good thing he came along because the plane caught fire just after that."

"Is the farmer lying?"

"I really can't say, he probably couldn't see properly, it was dark."

"So, were you awake and then suddenly unconscious?"

"I can't say as I remember Kommandant. I did have a head injury."

"What were you doing?"

"The plane had just crashed, I don't think I was overly concerned about doing anything much at all."

"If you do not talk, I can use other means to make you do so."

"As I understand it you're not allowed to do that."

"No, but who would tell?"

He smiled then, showing a darker side to his personality. "Schmidt." He called not taking his eyes off the Prisoner.

The door behind the prisoner opened and he turned to see a burly looking officer, with a mean look in his eyes, enter. The Kommandant told Schmidt in German he could take the prisoner away and do what he needed to get the information required, but that he wasn't to leave lasting damage, he was an officer and subject to prisoner of war rules of the Geneva Convention.

The prisoner pretended not to understand what was being said.

The Kommandant turned to the prisoner, "You will go with Schmidt. If you are lying Lieutenant, I will find out."

Schmidt grabbed him by the arm and dragged him out the office.

No matter what, he couldn't give away his secrets.

CHAPTER FOUR

Anna

"Damn it Forrester. What am I supposed to do with this?" Her editor was pacing the floor behind his desk, one hand rubbing his forehead. The dim afternoon light glinting through the windows.

"You can't have got nothing? Nothing!"

"I'm sorry sir. I did try. It was the reporter from the Sketch, he bombarded me with questions about the Leyac case and then some of the others joined in. I couldn't even ask the event organiser or the American speaker anything about the product and they left a little annoyed I think. I've put together what I could but it's not much."

"Forrester, that's no damn good to me. I have a column to fill and at the moment, my women's section is going to print with a blank space in it. It's just not good enough. I can't have my reporters coming back empty handed when they are set specific tasks. As it is, your personal life is getting in the way of your job and I can't have that. Maybe you should take a break."

Anna began to protest when he interrupted her, "And go see Marcus, he's planning an exclusive with the Leyac twin.

Might as well make the most of you, at least that's something we can do."

"Sir! I don't want to give an interview. I just want this whole thing to go away. And I don't need a break. I won't let it happen again."

He slammed his fist down on his desk, his face going red. "Forrester, you will give that damn interview. You've already come to me empty handed today. Don't make things worse or you will find yourself without a job. Consider this a warning."

"Yes, sir. I understand." She stood to leave, her face set with suppressed anger fists in balls at her side.

"I hope so for your sake Forrester," he said as she retreated toward the door.

How could he? And Marcus she could happily punch more than a few times. And that's without even considering the oh-so-helpful damned doctor, and then there was Julien Flynn. She still hadn't decided how to handle him yet. No doubt he'd be in touch soon enough but right now there was only one person she wanted to see.

She marched down the corridor toward Marcus' office and went in without knocking.

"Hello Forrester. How are you?" He said suppressing a smirk.

"What's this about an interview?"

She clenched her teeth as he casually leaned back in his chair surveying her through faintly smiling eyes. He slowly lit a cigarette and blew smoke toward the ceiling lazily before answering.

"It's going to be a great piece, exclusively to us of course. You ready to go, I've got questions prepared already," he began rifling through his papers.

"No, I'm damn not ready, I'm not doing it."

"That's where you're wrong Forrester. You don't have a

choice, not if you want to keep your little job, which I know you do. It's quite sweet really how attached you are to this office and how sad it is that you haven't yet realised you won't make it."

"What the bloody hell do you know about whether I'll make it or not. You really are a low life Anthony Marcus. And to think I was stupid enough to think you were my friend. You even fooled Doctor Laker. He thought you were interested in me."

He threw his head back and laughed then, "You are kidding. He really thought I was interested in you?"

Anna just glared at him, as she tried to steady her breathing and calm the anger she felt.

"Well he's off the bat with that one," he raised an eyebrow. "Anyway, we're getting off point," he said turning his attention back to his papers. "Sit down, we might be a while."

Anna sat, arms folded. She knew she had little choice but didn't like the way she was being forced into this. Surely it wasn't right to ignore her feelings?

"So, tell me Miss Forrester. Why have you remained anonymous all these years?" Marcus said adopting a professional tone.

"Marcus, you know the answer to that already."

"Yes. But I'd like it in your own words."

Anna sighed. "Damn it Marcus I just want this whole thing to go away. How is you printing more of it going to help? And, how do I know you aren't going to print something I don't like?"

"You can see the finished article and sign it off before it goes to press. How's that?" he said adopting the tone she had come to think of as being typical of him, but which she now knew was just the voice he used to get what he wanted.

"And you have no choice," he added placing his elbows on the table.

"I didn't know the truth until recently."

"Good, Miss Forrester, and what was it like learning the truth? How did it make you feel?" he made notes as he spoke.

"You really need to know that?" Anna moved her eyes to the ceiling away from his face but she could feel his expectant stare on her. "Shocked, numb. I suppose," she said suppressing the anger building again.

"So are you saying you had absolutely no inkling of the truth."

"Again, you know this already. None whatsoever," she said looking at his face again.

"So, tell me about your life, what have you been doing?"

"I grew up with my mother, we moved often. I went to school, got an education and became a journalist."

He put down his pen and leaned back in his chair.

"Forrester, if you don't start being a bit more forthcoming, I'm going to have to embellish details myself."

"Marcus. I don't want to…"

Marcus' phone began to ring and he stopped her mid-sentence with the palm of his hand raised while he answered it. He listened, looking up at her before speaking into the phone, "all right Sir, we'll be right there."

He replaced the receiver. "Come on Forrester, we're wanted. The Leyac estate have issued a statement in response to this morning's article. Let's go see what Flynn has to say."

"What?" Anna's body ran cold and she sat motionless for a few moments before rising to catch Marcus, who was already striding down the corridor.

The editor was sat squinting through cascading cigarette smoke at a starched crisp white paper. He briefly glanced up at them as they entered before returning his gaze to the paper.

"Come in both of you. Sit down. Marcus, hold your interview. We're running this instead," he flapped the paper at Marcus who moved to get it.

"What does it say?" Anna asked her heart hammering.

Marcus reads aloud in a mock upper class voice, "*The Leyac estate will not confirm any unproven claims made by Miss Forrester against the estate, and refutes the claims made in the newspaper article to any wrongdoing on their part. We will only consider claims of parentage, or rights to the estate on the production of evidence to corroborate that claim. Without legal proof of the identity of Miss Forrester and her mother, the Leyac estate will not view the claim as genuine and will instead look on the matter as a hoax.*

The estate will consider all claims where the party can produce proof to that end, on individual merits. However, all claims will be officially and legally investigated.

The estate was always in full support of the late Lord Thomas Leyac in his search for his twin brother and denies concealment with regards to hiding the identity and gender of the twin, and the whereabouts of Miss Forrester and her mother from Lord Thomas.

Miss Forrester should be careful as to any further claims she may wish to make.

Estate Manager and Trustee Mr Julien Flynn.

Leyac Estate."

Marcus stops reading and looks up laughing, "well he's still on top form I see. He's determined to hold onto the estate and money."

"Marcus, you know what he's capable of and what he said that day. Now he's threatening me. Did you forget, when you got greedy to make a bloody name for yourself, this is the man who kidnapped me, had me tortured for information and tried to shoot me, all to scare me off and keep me quiet? You bloody idiot, you've put me in danger."

"Why do you care what he threatens you with? He's got nothing, you have the proof. Why don't you take your birthright from him? Isn't that what your mother wanted in leading you on this journey in the first place?"

"No I don't think it is. I think it was to warn me, to prepare me for these people, so I could understand just who I was dealing with. Why would you provoke him like this when you know what he could do to me? He has a lot of power and a lot of money, all of which I don't. How the hell am I supposed to deal with a man like that. I can't believe you would do this to me. And you," she said turning to her editor, "you don't know the half of it, you only know what Marcus told you. You have no idea what you have unleashed."

"So, tell me then Forrester, let us print it. All of it," her editor said leaning forward in his chair and clasping his hands together on his desk.

"I can't do that Sir, it's too muddy and complicated. Telling the world just makes things worse. Isn't there more important War news to report."

"Ah, there's always War news, but a story like this takes their minds off Hitler and his threats. It gives them a bit of light relief."

"It's not light at all. It's at my expense. He could have me killed."

Her editor shrugged and Anna put her head in her hands.

"Forrester?" Marcus said quietly.

She ignored him and didn't look up but he continued regardless.

"You said Flynn has a lot of power and a lot of money, but you've got it all wrong. He has your power and your money. It's time you took it back."

Anna looked up at him just as he got up and left the room.

Anna left the office that evening feeling exhausted and wondering whether she'd had a worse day at work in her life. She was more than a little worried that Flynn hadn't been in touch directly. Surely this was not a good sign and the underlying threat in that letter was clear, as she was sure it was meant to be. So wrapped up in her thoughts, she found herself climbing the steps of her boarding house still considering this and with no real memory of how she'd got there.

She had just walked through the door when the siren began to wail, yet again, and Anna sighed in defeat. The day had finished her and she had no fight left at all.

Olivia came down the stairs, blankets and pillows in tow, her hair in pin curls ready for sleep, despite that it was only about six pm.

"Anna darling, what's wrong? You look frightful, what's happened?"

"You read the paper today?"

"No, I've been rushed off my feet all day. We had an influx of emergencies first thing this morning, a warehouse collapsed trapping a frightful lot of people who had been sheltering inside. I haven't had time to eat, let alone read the paper. Why what's wrong?"

Anna sighed, "I don't know where to start."

"Never mind Anna darling. I can see it's been a hard day for you too. Here take these. I'll run back upstairs, get your blankets and I'll grab the cocoa from my room. We'll sit and you can tell me what's going on."

Anna just stood there defeated as Olivia handed her the pile of blankets in her arms and dashed back the way she had come.

A short while later, huddled together in a corner of the basement slightly away from the others and the blankets arranged as comfortably as possible, Anna told Olivia everything as she sat sipping the hot steaming cocoa.

She glanced at Olivia as she finished her story, Olivia was holding her mug mid-air, a shocked expression on her face behind the steam rising and dissipating into the air.

The building shook and pulled Olivia out of her trance.

Anna left the office that evening feeling exhausted and wondering whether she'd had a worse day at work in her life. She was more than a little worried that Flynn hadn't been in touch directly. Surely this was not a good sign and the underlying threat in that letter was clear, as she was sure it was meant to be. So wrapped up in her thoughts, she found herself climbing the steps of her boarding house still considering this and with no real memory of how she'd got there.

She had just walked through the door when the siren began to wail, yet again, and Anna sighed in defeat. The day had finished her and she had no fight left at all.

Olivia came down the stairs, blankets and pillows in tow, her hair in pin curls ready for sleep, despite that it was only about six pm.

"Anna darling, what's wrong? You look frightful, what's happened?"

"You read the paper today?"

"No, I've been rushed off my feet all day. We had an influx of emergencies first thing this morning, a warehouse collapsed trapping a frightful lot of people who had been sheltering inside. I haven't had time to eat, let alone read the paper. Why what's wrong?"

Anna sighed, "I don't know where to start."

"Never mind Anna darling. I can see it's been a hard day for you too. Here take these. I'll run back upstairs, get your blankets and I'll grab the cocoa from my room. We'll sit and you can tell me what's going on."

Anna just stood there defeated as Olivia handed her the pile of blankets in her arms and dashed back the way she had come.

A short while later, huddled together in a corner of the basement slightly away from the others and the blankets arranged as comfortably as possible, Anna told Olivia everything as she sat sipping the hot steaming cocoa.

She glanced at Olivia as she finished her story, Olivia was holding her mug mid-air, a shocked expression on her face behind the steam rising and dissipating into the air.

The building shook and pulled Olivia out of her trance.

"Anna, darling, how have you kept such a thing a secret all this time? Why on earth didn't you tell me?"

"You have problems of your own with your Lieutenant in the POW camp. You don't need my issues clouding your already busy life."

"Anna, do you really think that would mean I wouldn't be there for you?"

"No, I know you would have, that's just your way, but I didn't want to burden you and besides, I didn't really want anyone to know."

Olivia frowned at Anna. "Well it makes little difference to me, you're still as annoying as ever whether you're a Lady or just an ordinary girl."

Anna laughed. "I'm never going to be a Lady. I'm just Anna Forrester, journalist. Well, if Marcus doesn't have me fired and nothing else goes wrong. Anyway, I'm tired of talking of this; I'm tired of thinking about it. I think my head might explode. For goodness sake take my mind off it. Tell me about you? Have you heard from him again?"

Olivia sighed, "Yes I have…"

"What's wrong? I thought this one was that special 'one' you've been looking for?"

"Don't say it like that Anna. I know you don't have a romantic bone in you, but I've told you before, just you wait and see," Olivia's face turned from a playful smile to a serious thoughtful expression, "but if I'm honest, I'm finding it odd how he seems to be growing on me now he's away."

"How do you mean?" Anna asked.

"Well, when we first met and he asked me to write to him

when he went back to base, I said I would as I felt sorry for him. These fly-boys have a life expectancy of six weeks and he was a sweet thing, so I agreed, but it was more out of pity than me actually caring for him in a serious way. It was to give him something to come home for. So, now he's written to say he's POW, I feel even worse, so have been thinking I'll write because he needs me more than ever. But…" Olivia paused. "… I can't put my finger on it, there's more depth to him than I thought he had when we first met. It's how his letters show he's a deeper thinker than the front he showed me when I met him."

"Well, maybe being a POW's changed him. It sounds like you've got yourself something special. I'm happy for you. Let's hope this war ends soon and he can come home."

"Let me read you his last letter and you'll understand what I mean." Olivia pulled out a neatly folded piece of paper slightly turning at the corners,

"My Dearest Olivia,

I hope this letter finds you well and you got my previous letter to say I was now a POW. It's too soon for me to have heard back from you but I wanted to write again as soon as possible. I hope you've written back and your letter is making its way here as I write this. I wait with anticipation each day the post comes in hope that there's something from you, even though I know it's too early.

I'm like a child waiting for Christmas, but honestly, there's little else to look forward to here. I miss you and home dearly and wish there was some way I could come back. I am finding that as the days shorten and the nights lengthen and the dark cold winter descends that I miss home more than ever, the thought of nice warm fires and warm blankets, hot strong tea from a proper teapot and homemade scones, are the stuff of dreams.

In my mind, I imagine the two of us in the summer heat, driving through the country lanes of Cornwall, the top down on my car. As we pass through a village, we and stop for ice cream and splash in a

stream that runs through down the centre of the village, before having a picnic of cake, and a whole mountain of delicious treats. In the afternoon we snooze in the sunshine. Doesn't it sound just wonderful?

But here in the darkness of the winter it is hard to see these things as anything other than just the fantasies of someone else's life, like fairy stories. When we're surrounded by war, can there ever be such calm tranquility again?

Do write soon,

Best wishes

Lt Johnson.

P.S. Send me a picture of yourself, so I can pin you to my wall and keep you close each night as I sleep below these stars far from home.

CHAPTER FIVE

Anna

Anna woke late the following morning. The bombs had stopped sometime during the early morning, she couldn't be sure when exactly, as she drifted in and out of a fitful sleep and a night of endless dark thuds. In her dreams, she was being chased by hordes of people, and everywhere she hid they found her.

She shook the memory from her head and pressed her fingers to her temple to disperse the headache thudding behind her eyes.

Olivia was already gone for her early shift at the hospital and Anna hadn't noticed her creep out.

She looked at the clock. She was late for work, but after the day she'd had yesterday, she thought she wouldn't be missed first thing this morning.

She got ready in an a trance-like state as the headache pounded behind her eyes and the desire to just crawl into bed and sleep blissfully was almost irresistible.

As she descended the stairs stepping over the worn bit of carpet and squeaky floorboard, something made her pause. Another small white square envelope sat on the top of a pile of equally square letters.

She crossed the hallway, the large Victorian door gleamed light through the criss-cross taped glass panels, and cast a pattern on the floor.

As she picked up the pile a flash of anger washed over her, sure enough, another letter from the doctor.

She thrust open the door and marched down the steps into the cold morning, smoke and dust lingering in the air and she could see large clouds of smoke from fires somewhere in the distance. The smell of plaster, dirt, damp and dust, again lingered in the air, but the sense of cold chill caught her when she took a gulp of morning air as she passed a man in a brown suit with his hat pulled down over his face.

Hadn't she seen him yesterday?

Despite the smoke, dust and damp, the air was cold, sharp and made Anna feel more alive, going some way to alleviating her headache. She never thought there would be anything worse than her beloved city being bombed to smithereens by the Luftwaffe, but her current situation was so much worse, that things which had concerned her before just didn't anymore.

When she got to the office, the place seemed in chaos and it didn't take long to see why.

"Forrester," her editor barked across the room as she entered.

She hurried to his office with trepidation of what he might want now.

"I want you covering a story," he said, "a big house on the outskirts of the city. The owners are using their extensive property to help those bombed out with nowhere to live. Go along, talk to the couple and those bombed out. Get me a good story."

Anna nodded, looking at the sheet of paper he handed her as she turned to leave. "And Forrester..."

She turned back.

"Don't let me down again. This is your last chance."

She nodded.

She caught the tube to west London. The front gates of the large double fronted house were big and impressive. A long, wide pathway led to an open square, at the front gravelled area of the property. Anna crunched her way up towards the house, her shoes making her progress slow but giving her time to examine the surroundings closely.

The numerous windows had criss-crossed tape all over, as did most places these days, but Anna marvelled at the amount of time and effort that would have gone into such a feat. The door had a large black handle. She pulled the heavy knocker and banged it, listening to its echo through the expanse inside.

After a short wait, the door was opened by an elderly looking butler, who peered at her through small eyes.

Anna explained her purpose and the butler gave her a slight bow and invited her in, instructing her to wait.

The hall itself was wide and square, with a number of rooms leading off from both directions and a huge sweeping staircase at the centre. Anna watched the butler disappear through a door to her right. The place smelt faintly of fresh lemons, mixed with expensive old fashioned perfume and babies. An odd combination and Anna wondered where the families were in such an quiet, eerie place.

After waiting for a while and wondering if the old butler had forgotten about her, a middle-aged woman breezed in with an air of confident exuberance.

"Oh!" she said when she saw Anna, "A woman reporter, how droll. You are the reporter are you not?"

"Yes madam, Miss Anna Forrester."

"Ah, Miss Forrester, why you're the Leyac girl. Ah well that's all right then. You're one of us. Come my dear, we'll take tea in the drawing room."

She kissed Anna lightly on both cheeks, drawing her arm through Anna's as if they'd know each other for years. Anna raised her eyebrows, this would be interesting.

"I must say, for all that I am happy in the work we do for these poor unfortunates, it is rather nice to speak to someone of one's own class. I don't mind admitting, now you're here, I was very apprehensive about your visit. I was expecting some dirty, smelly man who would poke his nose in everything, but now I know I'm going to be interviewed by Lady Victoria Leyac herself, that's all right. All right indeed. Tell me my dear, you don't mind my calling you Victoria do you. I assume you're taking up your name and heritage now," she looked over at Anna not giving her the chance to reply and gave her a little squeeze, "well of course you are. Can't let that dreadful little trustee get everything. It's simply not the way of things. Now sit my dear."

The woman had steered them into a large open room with two sofas facing each other at either side of a fireplace. There were large windows on two walls that looked out to the garden. The room was well-decorated, if a little fussy for Anna. The woman sat on one of the long sofas and leaned back but still managed to exude an air of authority. The woman's constant babble flummoxed and unnerved Anna now she had recognised her. If people were remembering her name, her own name, how likely was it she could continue as an unobserved reporter? She pushed the thought away. This was an exception. The woman was rich - she would naturally be interested in other families of the same standing, wouldn't she?

The woman rang a small silver bell on the table beside her and the elderly butler entered once again. "Oh, Barton do fetch tea. We're entertaining Lady Victoria Leyac."

"Now Victoria dear, let's get the nasty little business side out the way first so we can chat properly. What do you want to ask me?"

"Anna is fine, Madam."

"Oh, you poor dear, not used to the name yet. It will take a while, but you will never get used to it unless you practice, but I will humour you for today, Anna. However, the next time we meet, you must promise to allow me to call you by your correct name. And please call me Constance, I can't abide Madam, that's what Lord Lowcroft used to call my mother, lord, how droll."

Anna decided to accept this as she was certain she wouldn't be seeing this woman again, and the last thing she wanted to do now get into details of her current situation, so she stayed silent.

"So, Constance, what made you decide to open your house to bomb victims?"

"Oh, my dear Victoria, it was an easy decision. It all happened one night when I had been in the city for some bore of an event for my husband, he's a General and is very busy. Anyway, on the way home those dreadful Jerries began to raid and I had to leave my car in the street no less, and get into a public shelter. Can you imagine? Anyway, to pass the time, I got talking to some of the women and they told me what life was like. I don't mind admitting how shocked I was. Anyway, by the end of the evening I felt so sorry for these women I offered to drive them home in my car, they accepted with grateful thanks and seemed to think a ride in a motor car a frightful adventure, poor things. Anyway, when we pulled up at their street I'll admit I have never seen such a sight, whole rows of little houses smashed to pieces, it was unbelievable my dear. I have never seen such destruction. I don't mind admitting, it stayed with me. I see it now in my mind as clear as day. It was then my dear Vic… Anna, that I decided I needed to do my bit. After all I'm alone here in this rattling old house while my husband is off doing whatever he does. Why should I not help fight those blasted jerries coming here and bombing poor women and their babies. So, after some thinking I realised this was the best way I could help. And here we are."

She held her hands up in mock show of her surroundings, just as the butler returned with a tray and an exquisite matching china tea set. He placed the tray down and began filling the cups with tea from the pot.

"Barton, Lady Victoria and I will serve ourselves."

"Very good Ma'am" he bowed and left.

"How did your husband feel about the prospect?"

"He was most grateful for it, he praised me on my ingeniousness. I don't mind telling you because you're one of us, but the word is there are discussions of which stately homes will be turned over for use by the military, someone my husband knows tipped him off that ours was in the running, but now with this it's less likely. But that's strictly between you and I, don't print that my dear, it's terribly secret."

Anna nodded making notes. "May I see some of your new inhabitants?"

"Oh of course my dear but not before you've had your tea and we can chat properly. Tell me how long have you known the truth about yourself?"

Anna paused reaching for her teacup watching her reflection in the hot steaming liquid. She could feel the woman's gaze on her.

How could she steer this conversation?

What seemed like forever but was probably only 15 minutes later, full of hot liquid swirling around her stomach, she was ushered on a dizzying tour through the house of corridors, stairs and more corridors, to where the bombed-out families were now situated.

Down a darker, dustier, what seemed like a more unused part of the house, lay a long narrow corridor with doors on either side. The woman stopped. "Here is where we put the families," she said. Most rooms are of similar size but some are larger than others and those go to the larger families. I will leave you alone to get the information you require. Do come and see me before you leave my dear." With that she turned on her heels and left the hall, disappearing around a corner, leaving Anna alone.

Anna knocked on a door, the knock echoing down the empty hallway, the thud seeming intrusive in the silent empty corridor.

It was opened by a small boy with a runny nose, wearing nothing but his underwear. He stared at Anna wide eyed and she asked for his mother, an odour of damp washing lingering in the air. He continued to stare at her until a flustered woman in an apron came rushing up to the door.

"What are you doing you little rascal. Get away from that door." Then noticing Anna stood there, her mouth formed a surprised O.

To break the awkwardness Anna smiled. "Hello, I'm a journalist. I'm writing a story on the bombed-out families lucky enough to have been given shelter in this house. Would you be willing to answer some questions?"

The woman looked suspicious and instantly Anna felt her prickle.

"It won't take long and I've travelled all the way from the city." Anna said.

The woman pursed her lips, "Well, so long as you don't mind the mess of my doing the laundry, some of us work for a living."

The woman disappeared back into the room and Anna took this as an invitation to follow.

The room itself was large but had been divided down the middle by curtains to separate a living area from a bedroom area. The living area to the left of the now two rooms, had a huge fireplace that dominated the smaller area, but which would have suited the original large single room.

The small boy ran behind a chair, his large brown eyes peering at her from beneath its legs. The room itself was cluttered with laundry, and racks of drying clothes filled the room. The blazing fire, in the imposing fireplace, mixing with the wet laundry, gave the place a damp wet washing smell.

The woman had moved to the far side of the room and began folding a large sheet. She offered Anna a cup of tea as she continued her work.

"No thank you, I've just had my fill downstairs."

The woman shrugged indifference.

"I'm Anna Forrester, what's your name?"

"Mrs Lewis to you."

"Where in London are you from Mrs Lewis?"

"East End." The woman worked methodically and purposefully in quick deliberate movements.

"And what happened, how did you lose your home?"

"The bleedin' jerries, that's what happened. We was in the shelter at the end of the street with all the neighbours, and when we came out in the morning the whole street was just a pile of…well… Everything was gone, that's what."

"Where is your husband, Mrs Lewis?"

"I can't say as I know. He's in the Navy so best I can guess is that he's somewhere in the sea."

"You must miss him?"

"Not really."

The woman piled the sheets she had been folding on top of a stack of items and moved them to the other room.

"You seem to have a lot of laundry Mrs Lewis. Is today wash day."

"It's not all mine. I take it in ye see, for a bit of money, like I said,, some of us have to work."

"That's a good idea, to help make ends meet?"

"Hmm."

"So, how did you end up here?"

"My friend, next door. She'd been out the day the street was bombed, and sheltered further up town. She came back the next day, to find her house flattened, in the biggest car I've ever seen - well the only car - but that's no matter. Anyway, the car belonged to Mrs Fitzwilliam. She saw the state of the street and decided to help. Because it was my friend who was in with her, she made sure I got a place here."

"Mrs Fitzwiliam? You mean Constance?"

"Huh, well I suppose you would be on first name terms, you're all the same you lot."

"How do you mean, 'you lot'?"

"Mrs Fitzwilliam gives us her newspapers when she's done, so I know who you are Miss Anna Forrester." She made a point of spitting out her name like it was poison.

Anna went cold and she paused in her note making for a second before resuming and decided not to react, momentarily avoiding eye contact.

"You're all toffs." Mrs Lewis continued.

Anna felt her body tense and her face grow hot. This woman had no right to judge what she didn't understand, but equally Anna had to remember she was here representing her newspaper, so couldn't just reply any way she felt like.

"But Constance has been very generous. You are extremely lucky to get a place here." Anna said instead of what she'd really wanted to retort.

"Yeh I know that, but she's still a toff. Don't think I don't know she's only doing it to stop them taking her fancy house off her, tis nothin' to do with helping folk."

Anna was beginning to lose her temper; the woman may

have had a point about Constance's motives, but she was way too harsh. Anna excused herself and left, breathing a sigh of relief, as she went.

After talking to some of the other residents at Constance's home, Anna was pleased to say, although most were suspicious of her and quite tight lipped, non were as verbal about it as Mrs Lewis.

Maybe if she hadn't been exposed she could have got further with these women. Her identity being out in the world was really hindering her ability to do the job. Her editor's face popped into her head; she didn't want to think about what he was going to say.

Then there was Flynn. He had been unnervingly quiet about the whole thing apart from some letter refuting her claim, which, to Anna, knowing what he was capable of, seemed extremely tame and this worried her to a greater extent than if he'd been more hard hitting.

And all this was before she'd even considered the Doctor Laker problem - his face as he had looked at her that night, his eyes exposed with truth and frustration played like a scene in her head. She pushed it away. It was all so mixed up with her grief, she couldn't think straight.

On the journey back to the city, she squeezed herself into a corner of a packed train carriage and tried not to inhale the lingering smell of mud and damp wool that seemed to follow soldiers around everywhere she saw them these days.

Concentrating on her notes, she thought it more than a little interesting that Constance had been freer with her conversation than Anna suspected she would have, had she not thought of Anna as 'one of them'. It seemed that although the ordinary working women, with whom she had spent much of her career interviewing and writing about, now thought of her as an outsider, someone not one of them. But, in losing that she had gained the trust of something else.

She began jotting down ideas for her article. She could use this change and focus it on Constance rather than the women. Instead of a piece about the women carrying on regardless, she could focus on the generosity of Constance herself in opening her home.

She was deep in thought and almost missed her station, pushing her way to the front to get out of the carriage before the train moved on, feeling much more positive.

CHAPTER SIX

Anna

As she stepped through the office door and shook her coat from the sudden downpour, she could tell immediately that there was something wrong.

Her colleagues, although always busy and rushing around, seemed a little tense, a thick atmosphere in the air, giving Anna a sense of trepidation as she walked towards her desk.

Her editor, seeing her enter, came to the door of his office and just looked at her. The look on his face grim - arms folded, cigarette between two thin lips drawn in a tight line.

Without a word, she went towards him, he moved from the doorway to let her in and shut the door behind him, before moving back to his desk and sitting down, leaning forward in his chair at her and paused before speaking, "How did you get on this morning Forrester?"

"Good. Constance Fitzwilliam, the owner of the house, was very forthcoming I've got lots of good information about her and why she's doing what she is."

"What about the bomb victims?"

"Yes, I've got some on them too."

"Some?"

"Well, they knew about me and were suspicious and wary; bizarrely they saw me as one of the upper classes, which is ridiculous."

He sighed and rubbed his head with one hand, stubbing out his cigarette with the other, for once, not lighting another immediately and instead picking up a pen from his desk twiddling it between his fingers.

"Forrester, do you know what I've done this morning?"

"Sir?" Anna went cold with the feeling she was in some kind of trap, that no matter what, was going to mean trouble.

"I've been on the phone. There's nothing unusual about that, except I've been on the phone to people wanting to speak to you, wanting a statement. I've also had to kick out some of the boys from the sketch who came looking for you. I haven't got any real work done and now you come for the second time without a story."

"I have got the story, it's Constance's story. And Sir, I did say I didn't want the information released about me, for this reason. If you'd spoken to me first I would have told you this and frankly if you hadn't released that story this wouldn't have happened."

"Well for one, I don't just want the bloody toff's story, I want the other women too and don't you tell me what I should and shouldn't do with my paper."

"Sir I can make a good article out of this, and there's no one more frustrated with this situation than me. All I want is for things to be the way they were."

"The thing is Forrester, you can't get people to talk to you anymore. That was your big talent, being able to get the common folk to talk to you and that's gone now. You can't work properly because they're all interested in you. What am I supposed to do?"

"Wait for it to go away - it should do soon."

"That's just it Forrester, I don't think it will. It has all the qualities of one of those that captures people - tragedy, mystery, intrigue."

"You make it sound like a mystery novel."

"Exactly, that's my point. Forrester, you had the potential to be a good journalist. I could see you going places, even though you are a woman, but it seems you were to be someone who, instead of writing the stories, is the feature of them."

"Sir I can still do my job."

"That's just it Forrester, I don't think you can. And I can't afford to have anyone not performing on my staff. There's millions who'd have your spot in a heartbeat."

"Sir this job is all I've ever wanted to do. It's all I live for."

"I'm sorry Forrester, but I'm going to have to let you go."

"Sir, please don't; I can do it."

"Forrester, you have to face facts, you're a bloody lady toff, and you're going to have to go and do whatever women like that do. But out of loyalty to us, you must give us exclusivity on any interviews, etc."

"You're bloody firing me and you want loyalty?"

"Forrester, language like that from a woman is obscene."

"I don't bloody care. It's your fault, yours and Marcus' that I'm in this situation. You broke a story on me without my knowledge or consent. Where was your loyalty? Where was your exclusivity to me? How could you do this, when this whole damn situation is because of you."

"Forrester, get out of my office."

"I'm bloody going, I hope you are proud of your achievements."

"You need to control your temper. A lady doesn't get annoyed, not a decent one anyway."

"You really are a fool."

Anna stomped out of the office, slamming the door behind her, grabbed her coat and left the office without a word, a glance, or a goodbye.

She was fuming as she ran down the stairs and almost knocked over an elderly gentleman coming up the other way.

She apologised and took a moment to breathe, closing her eyes and willing herself to calm down, then descended the rest of the steps to the front door and stepped out into the busy Fleet Street. There were people rushing to and fro going about their work, and she stood for a moment watching, unable to decide what to do now.

This was all getting out of hand.

"Damn it," she said aloud.

"I'm sorry?"

She turned, to see those familiar eyes. "Hello Anna," Doctor Laker, said running his hand through his hair in that way of his.

Her heart lurched. This was all she needed.

"You don't look so well. Are you all right Anna?" He gently touched her arm but she shuddered, backing away. He removed it. She registered his disappointment.

"I've just been bloody fired."

"What? Why?"

"Because of who I am; because people won't talk to me; because they want to ask me questions instead."

"You mean that snake Anthony Marcus broke this story and now it's caused a ruckus you've been fired because of it?"

"That's about the sum of it."

"Well, I'm not standing for that. I was going to give him a piece of my mind as it is, but now…"

His words tailed off as he entered the building and ran up the stairs. It took Anna a few moments for her mind to connect what he was doing and she ran after him. He would just make it worse damn him. Here he goes again playing the protector, even though I haven't asked for him to.

He was taller and faster, so took the steps two at a time. She ran after him but the stairs seemed to lengthen somehow, seeming to take an age to get to the top.

As she entered the office she was in time to see the doctor speaking to one of her colleagues, who pointed in the direction of Marcus' office, a stunned look on his face. The doctor shot off again and Anna, ran along behind, the whole office now curiously interested in the strange goings on.

Her editor came to his office door, his woodbine clamped between his teeth, hands on his hips looking stern.

"Forrester!"

Anna sped past him towards Marcus office.

Marcus' office door was swung wide open and Doctor Laker blocked the doorway.

As she panted up behind him, she was just in time to see Doctor Laker's arm swing and make contact with Marcus's face. Marcus crashed to the floor knocking over a pile of papers, which scattered around him like confetti.

"What the hell is going on here Forrester?" Her editor's booming voice made her jump. He peered down at Marcus from over her shoulder and Anna could feel his anger.

"Who the hell are you?" he demanded of the doctor, pushing his way into the room and helping Marcus to his feet.

"He's the boyfriend," Marcus said rubbing his jaw with his hand.

"He bloody well is not," Anna replied.

Marcus snorted.

"You're a lowlife snake Marcus. You betrayed all of us when you printed that story," the doctor said ignoring the comment.

"Oh, get over it doctor. You're already the hero." Marcus said still rubbing his jaw.

"I'll bloody hit you again if you like," he said moving

towards Marcus again.

"I don't damn well care who he is, or what he is to you Forrester, get him and yourself out of my offices right now before I have you both arrested." Her editor's face was purple with rage and faint showers of spittle rained from his mouth as he spat the words at them.

Anna grabbed the doctor, the muscles in his arm taught with tension. "Come on, let's leave."

The doctor followed her but turned a few times back to stare at Marcus.

"I always knew there was something off about him, right from the first day, when I met him with you in that club."

"I remember you forcing me to dance, and quizzing me asking whether I was stepping out with Marcus."

The Doctor's face relaxed a little then, as a faint smile passed over it.

"Well you were completely off the bat with that guess," she said as they descended the stairs.

"He's still a snake who betrayed us, if you ask me," the doctor said, flexing his hand.

"Come on let's go get a cup of tea."

"Good idea." The doctor was shaking his hand again.

"That hurting?"

"A little," he said flexing it some more.

"That wasn't a very wise thing for a doctor to do, and while we're talking of it, you've interfered in my life again. I didn't ask you to play hero."

"No, but I can't help it." He shrugged as they stepped onto the pavement outside.

Anna's heart lurched. This was steering in a direction she didn't want to go.

"What are you doing here anyway?" she asked instead.

"You wouldn't answer my letters."

"You can't have come here just for that?" He said nothing

so she continued, "but that's ridiculous. What about your patients, your responsibilities."

"It's taken care of for a while."

Anna had remained silent in the hope of steering the conversation away from the only topic the doctor seemed to want to have.

By the time they had found themselves in a little corner café, with yet another pot of weak watery tea, and another wobbly table, they hadn't spoken a word to each other for some time, and the silence was becoming awkward.

"What are you going to do now you're not a reporter anymore?"

"Find another reporter's job I suppose."

"And how are you going to do that? Don't you see? You can't do that job any more."

"No I bloody well don't see that!"

"Well you're going to have to. You can't be a reporter while there's all this attention on you. You are going to have to deal with it all."

"In what way?"

"Flynn. You know how dangerous he is, you need to go and deal with this now."

"How am I supposed to do that?"

"Well the fact is the world knows who you are, so you now have no choice but to deal with Flynn. And, he can't do any more illegal deals to keep it all. He knows you have proof; he knows who you are despite what he says publicly. You need to go and take it back."

"It's funny that's exactly what Marcus said. He said I should take back what's mine. But no one seems to understand what I want. I want my life back. I don't want the inheritance or anything to do with that sort of life."

"You can't have your life back. You lost that the day your

mother died and left you that diary. It's about time you grew up and faced the fact that this is how things are and you just have to deal with each part as it comes."

"I bloody hate you sometimes. You always manage to say things that make me so mad."

"No, I tell you the truth. It's different."

Anna shrugged, sipping her tea and concentrating on the liquid in her cup and the swirling lights reflected on the surface, in order to avoid answering. She didn't know what to say.

"Anna, Flynn isn't going to let you fade into the background now it's out, and neither will the public. This story of the missing baby was a household mystery for twenty-five years. It won't just go away. Flynn knows that. You are going to have to go and face him. Deal with the situation and legally decide what you are going to do. You can't just hide in London. You have to go north and deal with it. You need some legal advice too. I know someone. I can put you in touch..."

"No don't worry. I think I know a place." Anna said thinking of her mother's letters to Toby Blackwood, friend of her grandfather Lord Ashton Leyac. She would try there first. He may have had someone take over from him.

"It's just... damn it all." She flung her hands up in defeat.

"Anna?" the doctor said softly.

She hardly dared look into his eyes.

"You know I'm right. And you don't need to worry, you're not alone, I'll never betray you. Ever," he said reaching for her hand.

She pulled it away and hid her hands on her lap beneath the table.

"You need to take back what is yours, then afterwards you can decide what to do about your career. Get your personal life in order first. It won't go away." He said moving his hands to fiddle with his teaspoon.

"I know," she said.

They fell silent for a moment.

"Anna there is another reason why I'm here."

"Don't doctor, I can't have anything else to deal with."

"That's why I'm here."

Anna opened her mouth to protest but he held up his hand. "Anna just listen please."

She closed her mouth and sat staring at her teacup again.

"I realise that as ever, my timing is as bad as it was the first time I told you how I felt."

"Doctor…"

"Anna, listen, this is the last time I promise."

She looked at him questioningly.

"I've come to realise that my initial belief that you loved me but just needed to see it, may have been mistaken. I thought I saw in you a reciprocation, but your determination to shut me out and your lack of response to my letters has made me realise that maybe you were in fact telling the truth, and if that's the case then maybe you don't love me and I was mistaken."

"Doctor…"

"Anna, I am here to say to you for the very last time, that I love you. I love you with all my heart and I want to be with you, but if you again today say you don't want me then I will leave and you will never hear me speak of it again. I won't contact you unless you contact me first and we will be as acquaintances."

"Doctor, I don't want to be with you," Anna said almost as a required response.

He reached for her hand then, "Are you sure?"

She felt the burning warmth of his hands and couldn't speak, so nodded her response. His eyes filled with bitter sorrow and pain, but he masked it well and stood up, nodding at her.

"Well then this is goodbye Miss Forrester," he said holding out his hand to her.

She stood and faced him, "Doctor, no not like this." She felt as if she was breaking to hear him speak so coldly.

He looked down at her, his hand outstretched. She took it to shake and he held it tight.

For a brief second he just stared down at her, then leaned forward and planted the briefest, most delicate of kisses and in a moment he was gone, a breeze of cold air replacing him.

Anna stood feeling the kiss on her lips.

What have you done? A voice inside said.

What I had to, she told it.

That was when she looked up and saw him again - the man in the brown suit with the hat pulled down over his face, and realised she'd seen him a lot; outside her office, at the station, near her house. Dread welled up. Was he following her?

Flynn. She knew it. Damn him. The doctor was right about one thing, she needed to take care of this mess.

CHAPTER SEVEN

Prisoner

Through the gap in the prison bars of the damp, dark and freezing hole he'd been in for the last week, the prisoner looked up at the sky.

Had it been a week? He'd lost track of time.

His ribs hurt to breathe from the 'friendly' encouragement Schmidt had given him to make him talk.

He'd resisted though, repeating rank and name as he'd been taught.

He could tell Schmidt would gladly go further but wasn't permitted. Really, he wasn't supposed to be doing this at all, but obviously the Nazi's don't care for following the rules, only their own, their invasion of everyone else's country told that on its own.

The grey sky held an air of sharp cold, as if a frost was coming, and he stuck a finger through the tiny barred gap to feel the morning dew drip onto his fingertip, and run down.

He couldn't remember the last time he'd eaten; he'd learned to ignore the pain. He had a terrible parched throat and licked the dew off his finger for some relief while rubbing his ribs tenderly, but even this made him wince.

The heavy wooden door behind him protested as the lock was turned and the door pushed open.

The prisoner squinted in the gloom, his heart lurching briefly with the anticipation of another beating.

"Get up," came the order but it wasn't Schmidt's voice

The prisoner got to his feet slowly, carefully peering at the shape in the door to make out who it was. Arms grabbed him and pulled him forward and out the door.

"Hurry up."

The prisoner stumbled as he felt the arms shove him again from behind.

Righting himself, he heard a chuckle and looked up to see Schmidt waiting for him at the top of the stairs that led down to the prisons.

The solitary area, which the prisoner had dubbed 'the hole,' had been constructed half underground, with the door and front area above a small set of steps leading down to the cells.

As the prisoner climbed the steps slowly, a rifle butt in his back, he tensed his muscles for a repeat performance.

He stopped in front of Schmidt, looking him in the eye defiantly.

Schmidt looked down on him amused.

"It seems the Kommandant is letting you go back to the huts with your friends."

The prisoner made to move past him but Schmidt grabbed his arm and twisted it.

"Make no mistake Englishce, I am watching you and when you slip up I will be waiting."

He let go of the prisoner and walked off.

Deciding then that he needed to escape quickly, the prisoner moved towards the huts and his bunk, which seemed the most comfortable thing he'd ever had at that moment, and started trying to formulate a plan.

And now that bastard Schmidt had marked him, he needed to get out before they dragged anything from him. No he would have to die first, and was quite prepared to do so, if necessary, although if he was truly honest, he'd much rather find a better way out.

He knew the escape committee but had, as yet, not been involved, preferring to watch and take stock of who he could and couldn't trust.

The escape committee could take ages and he needed to get out as soon as possible, but without telling Captain Smith, what the situation was. He couldn't see how he could get himself out through the committee in time.

It was better to go alone and the less people involved the better, he'd just have to make do and get as many things together as possible, things like papers would be the most important, clothes he'd worry about later. He'd have to see the forger and see what he could trade for papers, and to keep it quiet from the others.

The side fence behind the huts was a possible route out. If he could get at it, when the guard in the tower was looking the other way he could get under the fence. The difficulty would be the distance from the fence to the woods beyond. Once in the woods, he was sure he could find a way of evading capture.

He must concentrate on his planning and had no time for distractions; he thought of Olivia and a pang of guilt went through him. He had to carry on as normal but mustn't get too attached.

He had reached the huts now and pushed open the door, desperately wanting to lie down and sleep.

"Oh, you're back," Spiffy said, "I'll get Cap."

"No need," the prisoner waved a hand to stop him, the last thing he wanted was to sit and go through everything with the boys, but by that point it was too late and they crowded around him asking questions. Captain Smith peered from his office before walking down to meet him. Smith watched as he climbed gingerly to his bunk and laid down heavily.

"What happened?" Smith said.

"Well, let's say that Schmidt is a bastard and no mistake."

"What did he do?"

"Just a bit of a kicking, nothing I've not had from the boys on the school field," he tried to laugh, but his ribs hurt, so stopped.

Smith frowned, "but I don't understand why? Did he ask you questions, why you?"

"He didn't like my face Sir."

"Well that's not on, I'm going to take this up with the Kommondant, they know what they are and aren't allowed to do, and I won't stand by and let my men be treated this way."

"I appreciate it, Captain but it's not necessary, really."

"Nonsense."

He turned on his heels and marched out of the hut.

"Oh someone's head's going to roll now, he's hopping mad," one of the boys said, moving to watch Smith out the window.

"Bloody marvellous," This was getting worse, Smith had no idea what he was doing, damn him.

The Prisoner woke to early morning twilight, the cool rain vibrating off the roof and windows of his hut. The others were still sleeping, the heavy noises of relaxed breathing, the odd snore and shuffle as they turned over in bed. He moved to the window, forgetting for a moment about his ribs, until a pain shot through his side as he moved and made him suck in air. He peered out the murky window rubbing his eyes and stifling a shiver. He absently massaged his ribs.

The huge courtyard in the centre of the camp was rain soaked and the raindrops and puddles were bouncing up and around. The distant sound of thunder rumbled in the air, far away mixed with the sound of distant gunfire, but he couldn't be sure, whatever it was it wasn't near.

He looked up into the heavy pregnant grey clouds and the longing to get up in the air and fly home was almost too much to bear. In his imagination he could be home by lunch time and taking tea with a nice bowl of hot stew that afternoon, holed up in camp with the other boys. He missed it.

He would have to try and get onto the escape committee, just to keep all options open. He'd been trying to think of a way of going alone, but had realised that without at least one other to keep watch it would be near impossible. Plus, the forger wouldn't be budged on doing him an on-the-side job when he'd mentioned it last night. And, without papers, it was even more impossible. But, he hadn't completely ruled it out and was prepared at any moment to make a dash for it should the moment arise.

In the meantime, it wouldn't hurt to get on the committee. However, they needed to get to know him first, but he was sure he could do something useful to help the escapees. And in any case, this damned prisoner situation was a bloody inconvenience, if he was honest. And that's without thinking about what could be happening at home.

He pushed that thought away and Olivia came into his head. He felt guilty about her but was hoping he would be able to explain himself. He had been trying not to be bothered but her letters were a comfort and he quite liked the girl. He stood watching the rain for a while longer deep in thought and didn't notice the others in the room stirring, until the conversations in the room brought him back.

The others were chatting and joking around, while getting dressed in their various uniforms, or what was left of them. Many had lost parts of their uniform during capture. Some were missing jackets and one was even missing the shirt off his back. Jones he was called, and he was now wearing an old flannel shirt under his uniform jacket.

All in all they were a cobbled together bunch with various bits of each other's uniform, but generally they did try to keep their uniforms as correct as possible. However the Prisoner did notice his own was the tidiest, except for the faded blood stain that wouldn't wash out, a constant reminder of the other who had died that day. But, certainly some of the other services looked a bit more worse for wear than he did, but that wasn't half so bad as the Polish Army. They had been here a lot longer and their uniforms were decidedly shabby these days. The Nazi's tried to keep them separated, but the Polish seemed to be able to open any locked door or move around the camp unnoticed like thieves in the night. He and the others would have to pay attention to these men if they had any hope of escape.

His recent time in solitary following his meeting with the Kommandant and the delightful Schmidt had done nothing to weaken his resolve, if anything it had strengthened it.

The Prisoner slept walked through morning roll call, blocking out the rise and fall of the German speech about another failed escape attempt. The poor sods who had been caught were now doing a month in solitary, he didn't envy them that, but the chance of escape was worth the punishment of getting caught. The trick was not to get caught, but that wasn't as easy as it seemed by all accounts.

As roll call ended, the prisoners all dispersed to their various activities, some of which were quite enterprising, including language classes in German and French, a band of musicians, a chess club and even a drama group. The prisoner stood in the centre yard and surveyed the camp. When he had first got here he thought the place vast, but after getting his bearings he realised it wasn't as large as he'd first imagined.

The camp itself had started life as some kind of training facility, but had been turned into a prisoner of war camp by separating a few huts for the German offices, then surrounding the rest of the huts with double lines of barbed wire that came up about four metres from the floor, and a metre space between each row. One side of the camp had a large playing field, the other had a series of what looked like farm buildings, and a deep wooded area to the far side of the camp, down a steep overlooked valley. The front entrance led down a twisted road, which they had travelled up to get here, although the prisoner could not be sure from which direction they had come exactly, due to the monstrous headache he'd had that night from being smacked by something hitting his instrument panel during the crash, which sent glass and metal everywhere. The headache had lasted a few days and all through the period he was in the holding camp.

He had another letter from Olivia. It had been waiting while he'd been in solitary. The guilt he felt at his deception was only overpowered by his increasing thrill at receiving them. He was beginning to look forward to the possibility of another letter when the mail came round, and found himself disappointed and in a funk all day, when he didn't receive anything. He knew he needed to keep his mind on his job; he wasn't supposed to start liking a girl, least of all through a letter. He wondered whether it was possible to fall in love with someone through a letter, which reminded him of the old literature books he studied at university an age ago. Maybe it was possible, but the prisoner wasn't even sure he believed all that much in love.

He kicked his boot along the muddy, gravel and listened to the scraping sound it made. He took a swing back and kicked his leg out in a move he hadn't done since football back at university. He watched his imaginary ball sail across the camp and over the wire.

"Hey, Hey Johnson. Johnson!"

He didn't turn to start with but then realised that the speaker meant him. He turned to see Captain Smith coming up behind him. And nodded at him.

"Hey Johnson, with a kick like that, you should be in my football team, I'm looking for a striker. How about it?"

"No thanks Captain, I'm not much for the game these days."

"Oh come on, we need you, and it'll really get you in with the boys. Maybe it's about time you joined in - we're here for the long haul, so the Jerries keep telling us." He put on a mock German accent and stood more stiffly. "For you Lieutenant Johnson, The war is over." He then slapped him on the back and laughed hysterically at his own joke.

"Not if I can help it. Sir."

"Ha well then in that case you need to come and meet some of the boys. What skills have you got? But you must first agree to be in my football team."

The prisoner nodded his agreement. He needed to get in the escape committee and if a few games of football was what it took then that was what he would do.

"I'm a good planner and I'll make a good lookout."

"Excellent," the Captain slapped him on the back. "Good Man, good man," he then turned and walked away.

"When can I meet the boys?"

The Captain turned back and smiled, "Practice is this afternoon. 1400 hours sharp."

Clearly he was going to have to prove himself first.

CHAPTER EIGHT

Anna

Anna found the legal practice of Toby Blackwood and found it was now owned by an Edward Blackwood, which she presumed must be a relation.

The squinty eyed secretary behind the old fashioned desk didn't offer Anna that information and she felt no need to ask.

The woman peered at her through spectacles but turned away when Anna caught the woman's eye, all the while not stopping her rapid speed typing, the thunk, ping as she began a new line echoing through the silent reception area.

The place smelt of old dusty books and woodsmoke. A fire was popping and cracking in a grate on one side of the room. The office looked like it had started life as a townhouse and was converted at some point. It was a narrow building and the rooms led from one to another, a series of narrow rooms following narrow rooms, creating a long corridor building.

Anna crossed her legs and swung her foot absently as she sat, she wasn't really sure what to say to Edward Blackwood but she knew she needed some help. The doctor and Marcus had been right about one thing, she couldn't just hide he; she knew that. And now she had lost her job and burned the bridges of ever getting it back again. It was time to sort this mess out finally, so she could get on with her life.

A middle aged man, balding and carrying a little weight around the middle came out of the large oak door to Anna's right. It squeaked as it was opened, and Anna looked up to see him shaking hands with a younger man walking with a limp. This younger man was skinny, his clothes ill fitting and loose, he was unshaven and had a sad look about him, as if his life wasn't going well. Anna watched him limp towards the exit.

"Miss… Forrester is it?"

Anna met his gaze evenly, before standing to take his proffered hand.

"Yes, yes it is."

"Excellent, Edward Blackwood, pleased to meet you. Please come in." He stood aside and indicated that Anna should enter.

His office was cluttered with shelves and cabinets. Pictures, certificates and letters of different kinds all papered the walls. His big wooden desk stood in the centre and, unlike the rest of the room, was pristinely tidy. He moved round and sat, leaning both elbows on the des,.

"What can I do for you Miss Forrester?"

Anna, was only vaguely aware he had spoken as her attention was focused on the large painting behind the desk.

Realising he was still waiting for a response she forced herself to look back at his face. He was viewing her with an interested expression and followed the line of her gaze up at the picture.

"My father." He offered. "He began this practice and I took over when he retired. He's long dead now but he was an interesting character my father. Did you know of him?"

"No, not really. But my mother did know him and her

father before her. I believe my grandfather and him were particularly good friends in their youth."

"Oh really? What was his name, I may recall him."

""Lord Ashton Leyac."

"Ah, right. I knew I recognised your name from somewhere, you're the missing twin. But as to your grandfather, I can't say as I recall my father knowing him." A little frown crossed his brow as he thought.

"Yes they did, they were friends in their youth. He was with my grandfather when he first met my grandmother, Lady Eliza Leyac, who died in childbirth with my mother. But there was some kind of falling out after her death, due to, I believe, Lord Ashton's second wife Lady Catherine, and they were never close again from what I can gather," Anna paused watching his face pique with interest so continued, "however, my mother, in her youth wrote to your father and received a letter in return regarding the whole affair and detailing his side of the story, how things had unfolded as they did. You see, Lady Catherine, my mother's step-mother, kept the truth about Eliza from her and essentially sought to erase her rival from existence. Lord Ashton, by all accounts was so broken hearted by the loss of Eliza he took no pleasure or enjoyment in anything else for the rest of his life, apparently."

"How marvellously interesting. I take it you have proof of this story?" He said almost clapping his hands.

"Yes of course. My mother kept everything. I have proof of it all."

"And does this proof include proof of your identity perhaps?" He leaned forward then.

"It does indeed Mr Blackwood."

He sat back on his chair smiling. "So, can I presume you wish to officially claim Leyac estate?"

"No, I do not want to do that."

"Oh, really?" The surprise in his voice was clear, "then might I ask Miss For.. I mean Miss Leyac, what it is you wish me to do for you?"

"I want to know what are my options are. What can I do? Could I simply hand it all over to the trustee, for example?"

He stroked his chin thoughtfully before answering, "well all this depends on the proper production of the relevant documentation and that documentation being officially corroborated. But with that being the case, the estate will become yours as the next living heir."

"But then what? Could I decide to hand it over to someone else?"

"You may be able to if you wish to do so, although I can't understand why you would want to. Your brother, spent a very long time and a lot of funds searching for you and with him dead, you are the only living heir. You could do a lot for this country, the war effort and its people by taking up what is yours."

"Thank you Mr Blackwood." Anna stood to leave.

"I apologise Miss Forrester, I spoke out of turn, please do sit. I will not proffer unwanted opinions. You asked me for options, that is one."

Anna remained standing so he sighed and continued.

"If you wished to hand over the estate, you would first need to officially claim the estate and prove that you are who you say you are, then it would be a case of going through the proper procedure of handing over the estate to the trustee. Documents would be drawn up and you would need to sign them. It would be fairly simple."

Anna sat down thinking. He looked at her for a few moments before saying. "Although, if you didn't claim the estate and didn't prove who you were, the estate would simply remain as it is, but there would always be those who would work to find evidence that you are the Leyac twin. But essentially you could just do nothing."

Anna thought of Flynn, she knew he wouldn't let that happen now the secret was public. He would do something to get rid of her, she was sure of that. But if she claimed the estate and signed it over to him legally, then there would be no arguments.

"I can't just do nothing. The trustee, he is not someone you can cross without consequence so I need to make it official and give him legal rights to the estate."

"As you wish, Miss Forrester. First you would need to provide me with the proof to make the case that you are who you say you are."

"The proof is in York."

"Hmm, that is a bit of a setback but not too much, it will make the process longer."

"How much longer? I need this sorting out quickly."

"How soon?"

"A few days."

He laughed then, a big rounded chuckling sound. "Miss Forrester, that's just not possible."

"What if you came with me to York? I could provide you with the evidence you need and you can assist me in discussions with the trustee and whatever legal representation he has organised for himself. I believe it may be better for me to have my own legal representation, so things can be dealt with quickly. Is there any way you can dedicate some time to my case?"

"Miss Forrester, by all means, but there will be a cost, are you saying you would like me to act as your legal representative? Are you prepared for this?"

"The estate will pay."

"How do you know that?"

"Because, Julien Flynn is many things, but he always pays his way and he can hardly refuse to pay my legal costs when

I'm giving him Leyac estate."

"Perhaps."

"The estate's money is mine anyway, isn't it?"

"Yes, assuming the proof is verified."

"Well then Mr Blackwood, I will be in touch, we will leave for York in a few days. Will you be ready?"

"Yes, I'll make my arrangements immediately. I have some time off I'm due to take and my partner can handle things here."

Anna stood and left the office, breathing a sigh of relief as she walked down the street. She had asserted herself and it felt good. She finally felt like something good was happening and she was making progress to take back her life.

She could never go back to her old job, but there must be plenty of papers in need of someone like her, across London or even the whole country. She'd start looking immediately and once everything was organised and taken care of in the north, she could then get on with the important things in life.

She smiled as she went on her way.

CHAPTER NINE

Anna

The train journey north with Edward Blackwood was cramped and uncomfortable, the cold wind and rain not relenting as they journeyed northwards, spattering the train windows as they sped through the country. Anna watched the grey scenery from the window, thinking that she'd never spent so much time on trains in her life and she had taken the tube to work daily in London. Deep in her thoughts she was able to ignore Edward's snoring, his head laid back against the chair, mouth open, hands clasped around his middle-aged rounding stomach.

Servicemen in various uniforms crammed in and out as they moved through the country, getting on and off at different stops, some with kit bags some without, some in large groups, some on their own. The smell of must and damp wool lingering around them all.

When the train finally pulled into York station, Anna's heart lurched at the familiarity and the memories of the last time she was here. This is where things changed, where the doctor said those words.

No.

She wasn't going to think of him despite being unhappy about how she'd left things. There wasn't room for anything other than dealing with Flynn right now.

Leaning over she shook Edward's arm. He woke with a start, sitting rapidly and looking around confused. Blinking at her a few times, his expression slowly changed to one of recognition.

"We're here," she said.

"Ah, must have dropped off there for a moment or two. It was a rather short journey was it not, Miss Forrester."

Anna, who thought the journey had been long and cramped simply smiled and stood reaching above the seat to remove her brown leather suitcase.

They left the train and Anna led the way towards the bridge to cross over to the other platform, its curved arc swirling with steam around her ankles from the trains below. Anna glanced up at the arched Victorian ceiling and remembered that first visit here, when she had been rushing to see her mother before she died.

She pushed the thoughts away and sidestepped a mother pushing a large pram towards her, wondering how the woman had managed to get such a cumbersome contraption up the steep sweeping steps that led to the bridge.

As they descended the other side of the bridge that led towards the exit, Anna looked back at Edward Blackwood following behind, his long overcoat pulled around himself, hat pulled down at the colder climate. His face was set in professionalism and Anna couldn't make out what thoughts were hidden behind his blank expression.

Anna moved automatically towards the exit and the taxi's that would take them to their hotel, but she stopped suddenly and felt Edward Blackwood stumble into her as she stopped without warning.

He mumbled an apology moving beside her.

'Look,' she pointed.

She felt his head move and follow the direction.

'Ah,' he commented. 'It seems Mr Flynn has anticipated us, Miss Forrester," and moved past her towards the grey uniformed chauffeur with peaked cap who was holding a sign with her name on it.

She caught up with him just as he was discussing something with the chauffeur,

"My good man," she heard Edward say and the chauffeur turned towards a large shiny vehicle, opening the door and waiting patiently. She stood bemused for a few moments.

How did Flynn know?

That was when she remembered the man in the brown suit - he'd had her watched.

'It's perfectly all right Miss Forrester, this is Dawson, he's to take us to meet Mr Flynn directly. It appears we are to get straight to business.'

Anna got in the car, Dawson taking her case. Edward followed behind.

Dawson shut the door with a thud, making the car vibrate slightly. Anna ran her hand along the smooth, cool leather of the seat, the vehicle smelt of polish and wax, everything about it screamed luxury.

Once Dawson had stored the cases he moved around to the front of the car, got in and started the engine. The car roared alive, the engine vibrating through the whole vehicle and they moved off through the streets of York. Anna wondered where they were to meet Flynn, but as the car moved through the city streets and outside the city, Anna had the sinking feeling they were going directly to Leyac house

She watched the city streets descend to twisting rural roads surrounded by farmland, through villages and odd lonely cottages, a knot of anticipation at what was to come, sitting solidly in her stomach. She glanced at Edward Blackwood, who seemed to be enjoying the ride through the rural parts of the country. Clearly someone not used to travelling much outside of London, he seemed to be treating the whole thing as a big adventure. Although, she wasn't entirely sure whether this excitement was because he liked these dull, wet, muddy country places, or whether it was being at the heart of this Leyac mess she seemed to be in.

Deciding to ignore it, she glanced out of her own window at the wet, muddy lanes flashing by. She hated the country, and it smelt funny. She pulled a face at a clutch of trees that marked the top of a hill before they descended down into a valley and out the other side. She smiled at the memories of how her mother always came alive in the country and tears pricked her eyes, but she quickly blinked them away.

It seemed to take ages to get there and Anna was thoroughly tired and hungry by the time the car moved through the familiar village at the heart of the Leyac estate. Memories of her visit here, back when she had no idea what she was uncovering, and had simply come as a journalist looking for a story, floated through her mind.

How things had changed.

Anna pushed the memories away as she wondered whether her mother and Harry had walked together along this road.

All too soon the car was pulling along the tree lined way that led to Leyac House. The house flashed between the trees as the car moved slowly, painfully along, closer and closer to the gates.

As the car turned right and entered the large driveway, a young girl stood with the gate open for them and the car moved around the circular driveway. The sun came out from behind the clouds casting a warm shadow across the front of the circular lawn and the statue at its centre.

Anna's stomach flip-flopped.

"Well Miss Forrester, it's certainly some house, are you sure you want to give this up?"

"Let's just get it over with shall we Mr. Blackwood," Anna said stepping out of the car and looking up at the house.

This was hers.

The enormity of the knowledge hit her as she stood looking at the vastness of the place with different eyes.

The door opened as Anna slowly moved up the steps, her feet leaden. Through the heavy, oak door in the wide, square hall with it's cut-out ceiling up to the next floor, Anna paused.

"Where is Mr Flynn?" she asked the elderly man who had opened the door.

"Mr Flynn will join you in the dining room presently Ma'am." He gestured toward the door directly opposite the main front door.

Anna wasted no time, she strode over to the dining room door and opened it wide. The room was empty but the elderly gentleman ran around ahead of her and pulled out a chair. She sat. Mr. Blackwood followed suit.

"Luncheon will be served shortly," he said and left.

Anna sat uncomfortably irritated by this; she wasn't sure what game Flynn was playing. However, she was desperately hungry and secretly welcomed the food to come.

She glanced at Edward. He seemed perfectly at ease here and wondered how much help he would actually be, for the first time thinking herself foolish for trusting him without any investigation into who he was. Just because his father had known her mother and grandfather did not mean he was particularly any good.

As she was contemplating this, Julien Flynn strode into the room. Edward stood. Anna didn't.

"Miss Forrester I trust you had a pleasant journey?" He moved toward her taking her hand and holding it for a second, his own cool and smooth to the touch.

Anna suppressed the wave of hatred and nodded affirmation at him. Satisfied he turned to Edward.

"Ah, Mr Blackwood, very good to meet you."

"You have me at a disadvantage?"

"Flynn, Julien Flynn. Estate Manager and Trustee."

"Ah Mr Flynn good to meet you," he said shaking Flynn's hand vigorously.

Flynn moved around to the other side of the table, and sat, shaking out a napkin and placing it on his lap.

"Sit, I expect you are both hungry," Flynn said shaking a little bell on the table beside him.

The elderly man entered again with a younger woman, arrying plates of food and placing one before each of them.

Anna ignored the food, taking the time to examine Flynn.

He appeared oblivious to her gaze as he tucked into his meal.

"I must say, Mr Flynn, this is delicious, we haven't had such good food in London since before rationing." Edward said between mouthfuls.

"You are most welcome, Mr. Blackwood," Flynn said, "although it can be difficult for cook to source certain ingredients, we do fair better than the city."

Anna stared at them both. Was she the only one who thought this whole charade a waste of time. She had no intention of playing silly games, no matter what Flynn thought he was doing, but her stomach had other ideas as it growled and the smell of the food in front of her was intoxicating.

"Mr. Flynn…" she began as she cut her vegetables.

"But I must say Mr. Flynn," Edward began, interrupting her and giving her a brief glance, "I find this pleasantry rather unexpected. I did anticipate a rather more hostile reception."

Flynn showed no reaction, merely nodding taking the time to chew his food, while Edward waited for a response.

"I always find that things can be resolved much better on a full stomach and with pleasantries."

Anna scoffed, Edward glanced at her frowning slightly. Flynn showed no reaction.

"I quite agree Mr. Flynn," Edward said.

Flynn nodded, continuing to eat his food and without looking at her said, "Miss Forrester, is there something wrong with your food? Shall I have cook prepare you another plate?"

"No thank you. I'm not hungry."

"Tut tut, my dear. We can't have you not eating."

"Flynn, stop with all this nonsense," she said folding her arms.

"Ever eager; you should be more polite. It's a wonder your mother never taught you that." He said a note of viciousness in his voice.

Anna opened her mouth to protest but Edward interrupted her.

"I wonder Mr. Flynn, might I have a word with my client for a moment?"

"Of course you may my dear Mr. Blackwood, maybe you can remind her of the importance of eating meals. She should remember it's a crime to leave food these days." He smiled at her then, wiped his face with his napkin and strode out of the room.

Once he was gone Anna stood up and paced over to the large window overlooking the garden.

"Damn him, he's such an irritating idiot. He thinks he can just play games with everyone."

"Miss Forrester, you really need to control your temper and keep your comments to yourself."

"And why is that Mr. Blackwood? Who are you to tell me

what to do?"

"Because you've brought me here for a reason and I would like you to let me do my job."

"And how is exchanging pleasantries with that idiot going to help? It serves no purpose. I'm not here to play bloody games."

"Believe me Miss Forrester, I am in full command of the situation. Do not make the mistake of underestimating me. Let me do what you are paying me for. And part of that means keeping quiet and letting me deal with this negotiation."

"But that's the point, we aren't negotiating anything."

"Are we not Miss Forrester? Are you sure?" He paused, "Let me do my job Miss Forrester and for goodness sake, eat your food."

Anna nodded, she had little choice.

Satisfied he gestured that she return to the table, she did so, still frowning.

Edward picked up the little bell and rang it before forking in another mouthful of his lunch.

"You may tell Mr. Flynn we have finished our conversation and he may join us," he told the elderly butler who entered at the bell ring.

The man nodded and left.

The rest of the lunch went in a frustratingly perfect array of pleasantries - everything from the weather to architecture, in fact everything but the reason they were here, and by the end of the meal Anna was getting so annoyed she was quietly thinking she'd like to hit both men with a big stick.

"While this whole game is amusing, can we just get to the business of why I'm here, Julien Flynn?" She said purposely using his full name.

He looked over at her shrewdly, "Of course my dear Anna.

You were wise to represent yourself with a legal professional," he turned to Edward Blackwood, "although I have no notion of how you're going to do your job properly, she appears to want to interject herself at every turn."

"Mr. Flynn," Blackwood began, "I come here to, as you say, represent the interests of Miss Forrester and her claim on the Leyac estate."

"Thus far we are agreed, Mr. Blackwood." Flynn nodded.

"I didn't betray you Flynn." Anna spurted the words.

"Really? Well it is of no consequence now." He said caustically.

"I didn't. It was my colleague, trying to make a name for himself. I had no knowledge of it or I would have stopped it. I didn't want this any more than you did."

"Miss Forrester, that is of no consequence now, it is just important we deal with the situation we are in currently."

"Now Mr Flynn…"

"Can I stop you there Mr. Blackwood."

Flynn held one had up to Edward who nodded astonished.

"Let us not pretend that I, Miss Forrester and yourself do not know full well she is able to prove her claim to the estate and that she is the missing twin. Also, she could prove the existence of my knowledge at the bequest the late Lady Louisa Leyac and her mother Catherine. I myself can also prove that I was acting under strict orders from these persons and was also instructed to conceal the fact from Lord Thomas, which I did faithfully. I carried out my task dutifully to this family and followed instructions faithfully. Now, what I want to know is what your intention is, because I am not going to allow you, Miss Forrester, to turn my loyalty into some sordid secret."

"My client is still considering her position."

"No I'm not, I want rid of this damn house, you and the prison it's putting me in so I can return to my life and forget all about this bloody mess."

"Really?" Flynn sounded surprised and genuinely taken aback, he stared a few moments blinking at her before rising.

"As you wish, I will have the family solicitor draw up the necessary documents right away. In the meantime, it is important that you play your part. You will stay here and we will announce that we are in discussion about your claim."

"No I don't want to stay here."

"Miss Forrester, as I said, it is important you play your part. If you wish this to go away quickly then you must comply with my wishes. The estate will take care of your every need. Yours too, Mr. Blackwood, your bill and accommodation will be taken care of. I have taken the liberty of arranging transport back to the hotel in the village for you. Miss Forrester will remain on the estate."

He strode out of the room without giving either of them a chance to argue further.

Edward stood, "you must be careful Miss, that man is not someone to cross. And you really must let me handle him. I know what I'm doing. Otherwise it is a waste of my time being here."

Anna sighed. Edward was right, this was going to be very difficult.

CHAPTER TEN

Anna

Some hours later Anna had been shown to a room on the top most floor of Leyac house. The room itself was functionally, ordinary and clearly one that had not been used in a long while. In fact, it was quietly plain and shabby around the edges. It was completely unlike the perfectly kept and preserved rooms that were part of the museum tour. This room was small and had a narrow window that overlooked the front of the house. For a few moments she stared out, and down to the entrance gates below, before deciding she was damn well not going to sit here and do nothing all evening.

If she were stuck in this place she might as well do some investigating. She could look at the house with the knowledge she didn't have on her first visit. She shook her head at her thoughts of that time - some long-dead girl's diary, when actually it had been her mother. Back then she hadn't been allowed to look around freely - now however, the house was there for her to go where she wished.

What kind of journalist would she be if she passed up the opportunity to investigate further?

The matter of getting sacked would soon be sorted out

with a new position when she got rid of the shackles of this house and in the meantime, she could keep busy exploring and investigating.

Satisfied with her decision she dumped her brown leather suitcase on the bed and laid her jacket on top of it before moving to the doorway.

She looked down the corridor; it was dim and dark, a smell of stale air and a faint odour of damp lingered.

With a jolt, the words from Elizabeth's diary, as she finally escaped, came back to Anna:

When it was time to go, I fetched my bag, took one last glance around my room and opened the door to the dark, cool corridor and locked my room after me with Sissy's key.

My body was sore and weak and I confess, dear journal, to being desperately tired, however I could not help feel stronger with each step along the dark corridor. The sound of my breathing, the only distinct noise in the darkness, the air thick with anticipation.

At the end of the corridor I peered over the staircase down through the floors, to the darkness of the ground floor. Taking a deep, slow breath, I placed my first foot on the top staircase.

This was it. I had begun.

Tears for her mother pricked at her eyes making them hot and she rubbed her face angrily; she would not give in to grief. Not now.

But, this house just breathed her mother - she was everywhere - as if in the very fabric of the walls. She wondered why she'd not noticed it the first time she'd been here.

Within seconds she found herself standing with her hand on the door to the room that had been Elizabeth's, with little knowledge of consciously making the decision to go there.

She turned the handle and moved the heavy door open. This was the room where her mother had spent time as a prisoner. This is where she had been locked with her nursemaid, under the pretence of being gravely ill.

The large ornate bed dominated the room to her left and, as she stood, the diary pages came to life and she saw the room through her mother's eyes; not at the end when it had been a prison, but in the beginning, with the eyes of the young girl who had so much hope for the future.

A thick layer of dust made her sneeze as she moved to the dressing table and ran a finger along the surface - leaving a trail of shiny wood next to the grey, dusty surround, like a line made in sand.

The windows were shut tight, the air stale and badly in need of freshening. She worked at the latch but it was stiff and resistant, stubbornly unmoving. She was about to give up when she felt it shift. Giving it one final tug it squealed as it released. She pushed up the window to let in the cold, damp air, a fresh brisk sense of life entering and dispersing the sad sense of abandonment and loss.

The afternoon sun poked through the grey winter clouds and streamed in through the open window, bringing life and sunshine to the room. She looked into the distance, towards the village, and thought of all the times her mother had stood here looking out towards that same village, wishing for Harry.

The place was her, the room, the furniture, the way the ornaments were placed, the country view she'd always loved, the romance of a forbidden love, it was her mother, the place oozed her; it seeped from the very walls.

How could she not have known when she stole into this room the first time?

How could she have been so stupid?

It was obvious now, and Anna found the loss of her mother intensified just being here as if she was right there but just out of reach.

* * *

Anna left the room and moved down the wide staircase to the first floor, pausing momentarily in the round gallery to look at the large portraits of her family.

The door at the far end of the gallery led through to the drawing room and then onto the panelled walls of the long gallery, with its windows at either end casting light and shadow up and down the corridor room.

This is the place where Catherine fired all her staff Anna thought, remembering the description from the letter her mother had received from an old employee, when she'd been looking for Eliza Leyac. Anna wandered down a little way but stopped at a door left slightly ajar.

She peered round the doorway, into a tiny green room with a desk, which held neat piles of files and paperwork. The tiny room was covered in bright green wallpaper and had shelves with files on. The desk also contained a neat, shiny typewriter, much better than the one she'd used at the paper.

Was this Flynn's office or her brother's?

She looked behind and seeing no one around, went inside and shut the door.

The feeling of intrusion was only quietened by her sense of curiosity at what secrets Flynn might have hidden here, and more importantly, what he was up to.

And, besides, technically the place was hers so she could look where she liked.

Moving to the desk front, she opened the drawers and leafed through stacks of paperwork, some were staffing bills, some were receipts, nothing interesting just household account information.

She moved to another drawer, this was filled with ledgers that were neatly kept and recorded different transactions in an impeccably need hand. She closed the drawer.

The very bottom drawer of the desk was locked and had a

key hole. She looked around for its location beside underneath and around the desk top but found nothing. Sighing, she put her hands on her hips and looked around. She moved to the bookshelves looking intently at a small framed picture of her brother in what looked like a fishing outfit with a rod slung casually over his shoulder.

She picked it up for a closer look and a little clink noise of metal hitting wood caught her attention as something behind the picture fell on the floor. Looking down, it was a tiny gold key.

She picked it up smiling,

"There you are."

She went back to the drawer and unlocked it. Inside there was a brown envelope with private written on the front in big official letters. It had no postal address and looked as if it had been hand delivered.

Ignoring the private mark. Anna opened it and read the letter inside.

Dear Mr Flynn,

Further to your enquiry I can confirm I have discovered the details of the circumstances surrounding Captain Leyac's death. As ever, though, you must ensure this goes no further.

As we discussed at our last meeting, he was indeed in Germany leading up to his death, however, I cannot tell you what he was doing there as this is beyond my clearance Level, but the plane crash that caused his death is genuine - he was at that point returning home.

I don't need to stress that it's only because of our previous friendship and how much I know you've always cared for Leyac that I'm giving you this information.

It must be kept secret.

But, I hope it will go some way to give you a way to move on.

I am sorry to say it wasn't a pleasant end, and if you'd rather not know, stop reading and burn this letter immediately.

I knew you'd keep reading, you never could stand to be in the dark.

Well don't say I didn't warn you.

It seems Captain Leyac was picked up in Germany at some point between 1.30am and 2.00am that morning, I haven't the information on location but the plane took off successfully. However, as they reached the border of Germany heading west, they were spotted by a German fighter and shot at. The plane was damaged and the pilot had to emergency land in a field. The pilot got himself out in time before the plane caught fire but, unfortunately Captain Leyac did not. However, it's widely assumed he was already unconscious or dead from the crash so wouldn't have suffered.

The Pilot, Lieutenant Johnson, was captured and is now a prisoner of war, so we're unable to ascertain his side of the story at present, but as we understand, it would have been very quick and Captain Leyac wouldn't have known a thing.

I am sorry the information is vague but that's all we have. I can't stress again how important it is you keep this to yourself.

Do look after yourself.

Regards, Your friend

W. Gardener.

Anna read the words again, could it be? Surely there's more than one Lt Johnson, it couldn't be Olivia's Johnson, could it?

But how many Johnsons just happen to be RAF and just happened to have had their plane shot down and just happened to be in a POW camp.

He was the one.

He was the one who knew what really happened to her brother and how he'd died - and he was Olivia's Johnson.

The thought of her brother being burned, possibly burned alive was almost too much to think about. She wondered how Flynn had reacted. This W. Gardner seemed to think he'd cared a lot about him.

Anna thought of Olivia, how would she take the news her beau being the one who was flying the plane that killed her brother. Anna wasn't looking forward to telling her that.

Maybe she shouldn't tell her at all.

Olivia had a lot going on and her job was not the easiest, plus it was true, Anna had noticed her looking drawn and tired in recent weeks.

But if she said nothing Olivia would be extremely angry. Then there was the problem that the information in this letter wasn't even legally open to public knowledge, even Flynn shouldn't have it.

Then there was Johnson himself, how would he like to be discussed in this way, and particularly with regards to his own experiences, he may not like to have his girlfriend told what had happened.

Anna decided she would bide her time for a little while and first get through the ordeal of dealing with Flynn and this millstone of a house.

Either way, she was keen to wrap things up and get back to London and her career. She wasn't sure how she was going to salvage it but she just had to find a way.

Tucking the letter away again and locking the drawer she replaced the key behind the picture and heard the faint sound of footsteps coming closer. Her heart pounding she slipped out of the room and moved towards the library on the opposite wall, just before the elderly butler entered the long gallery and carried on past, entering the rooms that led to what used to be Catherine's chambers.

She breathed in relief and dashed back to her room.

CHAPTER ELEVEN

Prisoner

Johnson had been in the football team for a week and had been getting on well. He had begun to remember just what it was he had liked so much about it during those long days at school, days that seemed to be memories from someone else's life now he was here in the camp surrounded by Nazis.

He put his boots on quickly that morning, wiggling his toes to return the feeling to the numb-ends and rubbed his hands together to bring back some warmth. Moving nearer to the central burner he stood next to one of the other lads, also doing the same thing. The winter had really begun to set in and he was sure it was going to be a bad one this year.

"All right, Johnson?" The other prisoner said nodding at him.

"Bit bloody cold this morning. Frank" he said rubbing his hands together to stave off some of the cold.

"Eye, winter's here. How's that girl of yours?"

"Not bad, I'm hoping for another letter in the next post run."

"Yes, me too, my wife's joined the auxiliaries, Thinks she's helping us like," he laughed.

Johnson nodded and they stood in silence for a few moments both lost in thought, then Frank nudged his arm and looking up he followed Frank's gaze.

On the bunk to the left of them, a young soldier, really young, in fact he looked 17, although he said he was 18, had been caught a few days back. For some reason he'd been brought here, but they weren't sure why, since he was an Army lad and these were Officers' camps. It was either a mistake, or the Jerries didn't know where to put him.

He didn't think they'd make a mistake, so it must be that there was nowhere else for him to go and he'd probably be moved on shortly.

Some of the others had enjoyed having a young lad to boss around, but the boy was defiant and didn't like taking orders from RAF, besides he seemed a bit unhinged and Johnson made a point of telling the others to just leave the lad alone.

They looked over at him, now he was rocking slightly on his bed, staring into nothing and muttering things under his breath. Johnson glanced at Frank who gave him an amused shrug.

"Barking that one," Frank said.

When they all filed out for roll call, Johnson found himself on the front row with the young soldier next to him.

Stamping his feet a little to keep warm and blowing on his hands he glanced over at the young lad. His face was pale and he was staring straight ahead, eyes wide.

"You all right?"

The boy didn't seem to hear, so Johnson repeated the question. The boy glanced at him a shocked expression on his face, as if he hadn't known there was anyone else there, and blinked before opening his mouth, then closing it again.

"You don't look well, you feeling ill?"

"No, I'm fine. I just don't like being confined like this."

"Join the bloody club, lad. None of us likes it."

"You don't understand, I need to get out, I need to get out now."

"Why?"

"I just can't stand it, I can't stand it," the lad had now started shuffling around agitatedly and rubbed his face with his fist.

"It's all right, just keep quiet, we'll talk later. You're going to draw their attention if you keep talking like that."

"No I mean I've got to get out now."

"Now, how do you mean now?"

"Oh shit I can't stand it, I'm going, I'm going now over that fence."

"Don't be stupid, you'll get yourself killed. They'll shoot you dead before you even reach the fence."

"I don't care, I'm going."

Johnson grabbed the lad's arm and held it there, "Just stay where you are," he commanded.

He loosened his grip when he felt the lad's muscles relax and calm, but within a second he had shot off ahead at a sprint towards the fence. There was an intake of breath from the rest of the group as they watched him run for it, all knowing what was coming, but hoping that just maybe, just maybe…

"Halt!"

"HALT!"

The repeated shouts for him to stop fell on deaf ears as he continued his dash for freedom.

"Halt or I will shoot."

The lad continued, he was almost at the fence now.

Could he actually do it?

Please let him make it.

"Halt."

He was at the fence and began to climb when the shot rang

out echoing around the camp. Johnson felt the exhaling of breath all around him at another defeat. They had all known, but there is always hope; hope, when they had nothing else left.

The lad fell to the floor, a wound from his shoulder seeping blood into the gravelled ground beneath him.

The notorious Schmidt walked up to the lad, now moaning and writhing in pain on the floor.

"You did not halt when told," he said stamping his boot onto the lad's wound.

The boy screamed.

"That is for not doing as commanded."

He moved round to the other side, the boy gasping for breath and Schmidt leaned over the writhing body.

"This is for being stupid," he kicked the lad in the side who gasped again as the wind was knocked out of him.

He then crouched down and began stroking the boys hair, shushing him, "And this," he said pulling out a large curved knife, the boy's eyes going wide, "is for being British."

Schmidt slit the boys throat in one swift movement, a chocking, gurgling sound escaped as blood oozed from the wound pooling on to the dirt below, and the boy's body jerked before lying motionless.

Schmidt stood smiling, satisfied. "This is what happens to those who defy the Reich," he said standing over the body.

The Kommandant was stood at the door to his office and shouted Schmidt to come. He did so leaving the rest of the Nazi officers looking around stunned.

The prisoners stood together silently. They knew that what Schmidt had done was against rules, but were stunned that he had the gumption to do it. The rules of officer treatment, apparently, didn't matter here, but then the lad wasn't an officer.

"Back, Back, Back to your huts now," the remaining guards

shouted.

The prisoners followed one another all in stunned silence, each realising that if any had forgotten the guards were the enemy, they'd had a sharp, short, wake-up call that morning.

Johnson still felt the touch of the lads uniform beneath his hand.

Could he have stopped this?

He was just a boy.

The scene played over and over in his mind. The blood. The boy's words. His face. The smell.

The smell of death.

Damn him the fool boy

Following that day he spent much of his time angry, pacing the camp perimeter like a caged bear, over and over.

He'd been to Captain Smith and asked to be bumped up the committee escape list, but had been told he needed to wait while they organised their next move, and that there were people ahead of him with more important needs.

Frankly he was impatient and fed-up. He'd decided that going alone despite it being far more risky, and having less chance of success, might be the only way he could get out.

There was a wagon that came as regularly as clockwork, with supplies each week and he knew that if he could get on the work detail that unloaded it, he might be able to stow-away in the wagon when it left.

He knew he was risking another spell in solitary, but the thought that just maybe it might work. It was too tempting not to try. He didn't have time to wait, he wanted out - no he needed out - now.

There wasn't time for turn-taking and waiting around for Smith to be diplomatic - they just didn't understand his situation.

He'd noticed Schmidt had been watching him with a look

as if he couldn't decide whether to take him for another beating or not, which was pretty unnerving.

He needed to focus.

After a bit of haggling he managed to get himself on the work detail for the next day and he laid awake going over his plan.

He was sure it could work. He'd worry about papers and clothes once he was clear of the camp.

One step at a time.

He awoke with a start as the noise of stirring filled the room.

Today was the day, and he pushed down his nervous excitement.

As he and the others on the work detail filed out to unload the supply wagon, he pulled his hat lower and hunched his shoulders to disguise himself as they passed Schmidt's henchman.

The wagon unloading went well, and as they were carrying sacks into the storeroom, he paused and whispered to Frank, "Cover for me will you."

Frank looked up sharply, "What are you planning?"

"Can you distract the guards?"

"Yes. Does Captain know about this?"

Johnson shrugged.

"You sure you know what you're doing? Captain Smith will be boiling mad if you fail - going against the committee."

"I'll take that chance," he said plopping the sack down on top of another and straightening up.

"Alright then," Frank said shrugging.

Johnson patted his shoulder, "thanks."

Frank nodded and left. Johnson followed.

They unloaded the last few items off the wagon and Johnson hung around at the end near the back of the wagon.

Frank was taking the last sack to the store when he feigned

dropping it, splitting a corner so grain spilt out on the floor.

"You idiot," a guard shouted and smacked him across the head with his rifle butt.

Now was his chance.

While everyone was distracted by the spilt grain, he jumped onto the wagon and covered himself with some old plastic behind the now empty boxes.

He listened to the commotion as a few more were roped in to help clear the mess and he listened as they marched back to the camp area.

It was then he felt the engine of the wagon start and it juddered away, vibrating through his body. Johnson held his breath. It gained a little speed and turned a corner towards the main gates.

He listened, his ears straining.

He was nearly there.

He felt the wagon start to move faster but then heard a shout and the wagon stopped again suddenly. He heard a thud and felt a movement as booted feet landed on the wagon floor near him and began walking.

Suddenly the plastic was torn away and a rifle was aimed at his head.

"Up!"

He got up slowly, hands in the air and moved to the end of the wagon cursing under his breath.

He jumped down to a sea of rifles aimed at his head and in the centre was Schmidt, a cruel smirk on his face.

"Nice try, Englische," he said adjusting his gloves and moving slowly towards him.

"Very nice try." He was now face-to-face with him and Johnson held his gaze.

Schmidt turned away and moved a few steps, swung round, raised his fist and smacked Johnson square in the jaw with one mighty blow.

He stumbled backwards in surprise as the searing pain shot through his face.

Schmidt laughed aloud, "All you have done Englische is get yourself a ticket to solitary in my company, and I will make sure your stay is even more pleasant than last time."

He walked away laughing.

"Take him away," he said over his shoulder.

CHAPTER TWELVE

Anna

Anna spent much of the meal watching Flynn trying to work out his intentions - this was the man who had her kidnapped and shot at her. She had no doubt the niceties would end soon enough.

Then what? a voice asked her, but she pushed it away and ignored the thought, concentrating on her food and trying not to let it show just how nice it was.

Flynn and Edward spent much of the meal talking about war progression and how things were going. Anna sat in silence until she could hold back no longer.

"So, Flynn, tell me about my brother."

She saw him visibly stiffen, his face frozen in neutrality and she knew she'd hit a nerve. The awkward silence that followed made Anna, for the first time, feel as if the tables of power had somehow shifted in her favour.

Composing himself and making a point of taking a sip of his tea he said, "What do you want to know?"

"Well simply who he was, what kind of person he was. What was his favourite food?"

Flynn opened his mouth to speak and Anna butted in

before he had chance to finish, "What kind of master was he to you?" she said pointedly, highlighting he was the servant, not the master.

His fork stopped suddenly midway between his plate and his mouth before he put it down slowly and dabbed his mouth with his napkin. Leaning back in his chair he smiled at her shrewdly, "Oh the best, the absolute best Miss Forrester. Do excuse me."

He got up and left the room.

Anna smiled after him, something had definitely shifted.

During the evening she wandered around the upper floors of the house, through the gallery looking at the portraits of the Leyac family, all except her mother and grandmother. Catherine's was there of course and she stared at the shrewd icy blue eyes for a time, wondering what it was about that woman that made her go to such lengths - to kill Sissy. Then Louisa, a prettier, more softer version of Catherine with a certain wildness about her.

Then there was Lord Thomas, looking ever the regal gentleman. His dark blond hair had a wave to it, and his eyes, although commanding, looked kindly.

She felt an odd sensation looking into his face with the knowledge here he was her twin. This is whom she had been missing all her life and this was a man whose body had burned. She thought of the flesh twisting and deforming and shook the image from behind her eyes.

She looked up into his intelligent eyes and didn't quite know whether she was sad, happy or annoyed about everything. She wondered what he would have said about her had he been here.

Would things have been easier?

Anna left the portraits and moved down the long gallery

towards the library, firmly staying away from the green room. The door to the library was open and she sidestepped a sign intended for visitors marking its entrance.

Inside, just like the first time she was here, there were roped areas marking where visitors could view the room but not enter and peruse the books. Anna looked at the rope, paused for a few moments then stepped over it.

The thought hit her then, that this library, these books, these rooms, were hers - if she wanted them.

She pushed the thought away, remembering all the trouble it had caused and began scanning the shelves for something to take up to read in bed - she really needed something distracting to help her sleep.

She scanned each title with her finger, skipping the ridiculous romance ones, they didn't interest her, although she remembered her mother's love of Austen, a love she'd never shared, being more of a mystery reader herself.

Her hand moved on, then her thumb rested on a small green volume. That's the one she thought, gothic horror in the form of a monster, and this, she thought, is the perfect place to explore such a story.

Returning to her room she snuggled herself down in the thin blankets, quietly relishing the opportunity to sleep in a bed once again, rather than a damp cellar floor and the silence she was finding hard to get used to. It reminded her of clearing her mother's cottage in Abbeyfleam and she made a mental note to write to the Baxters' and Olivia tomorrow morning and catch up.

She noticed that someone had delivered her hot cocoa while she had been in the library and she wasn't sure whether to be happy or unnerved.

She sipped the steaming mug, thinking of Olivia for a moment, wishing she were here. Replacing the cup on the table she opened her book, settling down on her pillows to read.

But she was little more than a few pages in when her mind wandered to other things, those portraits downstairs and the faces of those now gone, kept swimming though her mind, no matter how hard she tried to concentrate on her book.

Sighing she closed the book and discarded it, annoyed. She picked up her cup and began sipping it again.

This would be a long night.

That's when it hit her, the portraits - that's what's niggling her.

In Elizabeth's diary she had said something about Eliza's portrait being in the attic.

Would it still be there?

Could she see the face of the woman who had been her grandmother?

Anna got out of bed and threw on her dressing gown robe. She scanned through the drawers and cupboards until she found some candlesticks and matches. She smiled satisfied, it was unlikely there would be any light up there.

She opened her door quietly. According what she remembered from the diary, the stairs to the attic were at this end of the house.

She peered up at the round window of the hall, blacked out, it's circular form hidden beneath the fabric so only the dim outline peered through.

Yesterday, while roaming through the treasure trove that is the attics of Leyac House, in search of clues, old pictures, letters, anything to aid my investigation, I arrived upon a large flat wrapping which appeared as if it could be a portrait of some kind…

Anna quickly found the small wooden door that led up the attic stairs and opened it. Slipping inside, while feeling inside her pocket for the matches, she struck one and lit the candle. To her right was a small cupboard with a candlestick and an oil lamp on it. She took the candlestick and pushed her candle towards it until a flickering beam appeared, lighting the stairway a little more.

Looking upwards into the gloom she gingerly tried not to put much too weight on each step, as she slowly moved upwards, dust and cobwebs floating on the air like a thick fog and sticking in her throat.

No one had been up here for years.

She wondered if anyone had been up here since her mother had all those years ago, but dismissed the idea. Of course, someone must have.

At the top of the stairs the attic stretched out before her, the gable of the roof line descending at either side and the attic itself stretching out wide, lengthways, in a large rectangle that she could just make out under the candlelight.

She tried to remember what it was Elizabeth had said. She had mentioned the picture was hidden somewhere behind some large heavy things.

What were they?

She moved towards a collection of furniture and squeezed behind a unit, where she spotted the covered sheet of a large flat package.

That was it.

Wasn't it?

It was tucked beside some furniture and was heavy as she dragged it, wondering how her mother had managed to drag it out herself.

Pulling, inch by inch, she heaved the object out from its hiding place, the dim candlelight flickering off the walls and furniture, giving the place a distorted feel. Clouds of dust flew like a sand storm, making her cough.

Once she managed to pull the object out of its resting place, she leaned it against a large dresser and sat back on a wooden bench opposite, just looking at the parcel in the flickering candlelight.

She wanted to rip it open but at the same time, was scared it wouldn't be what she was looking for.

After a long time Anna stood, rubbing her sore fingers and began ripping off the wrappings. They resisted and she cut her fingers trying to rip them open. After a lot of pulling and ripping the wrappings came loose and she stared into the face of a dark-eyed, curly-haired beauty, with porcelain skin and a hauntingly captivating face.

Anna just sat and looked at the picture for a long time. She could see her mother, but equally this face had a more elfin-like quality. The hair was her mother's, she recognised it straight away; the eyes too were the same but that was it.

In that moment Anna felt a strange sense of her mother, as she remembered her description of when she had found the portrait and how those words seemed to shorten the distance of time, and yet lengthen it too, so that her mother seemed further away than ever, but also closer somehow, as Anna mirrored the footsteps she had taken many years before.

It was a shame such a beautiful portrait was hidden up here, and had been for so many years; it should be on display, but that was none of her concern, Flynn was in charge. A sense of annoyance washed over her at that thought, but she pushed it aside, smiling at how she'd found a weak spot in his perfect facade earlier that day.

As she pulled an old blanket over the portrait to protect it. She noticed it had exposed a stack of boxes and things hidden behind.

Anna heaved the first box down and opened it.

Inside was a vast array of ornaments, silver boxes and unusual statues all piled up haphazardly.

A stack of letters were tied into a bow, dusty with age. She opened the ribbon and took the first letter, it was addressed to Lady Eliza Leyac and had come from the Far East. Anna remembered that Eliza's father had been a military man and she had grown up in one of the commonwealth countries.

She opened the letter, faded with age and a scrawling hand that was difficult to make out in the dim flickering candlelight.

My dearest Eliza,

How are you settling in to your life in dreary England, married to a ridiculous lord?

I for one, wish you would just leave and come back to Africa, I miss you terribly and can't seem to find a thing to do. My life is one endless array of bored days, stiflingly hot and dull.

Oh my dear Eliza please come back to me, you are the one thing that makes life here bearable and I just can't manage it alone. I told the olds that they should have let you come back, but you know your father - always looking for the next promotion or social scale to climb. Personally, I find the whole thing tedious.

Oh Eliza, forget this playing at being wife, do come home to me. I can have your ticket sent through directly.

Your loving and dearest George.

Anna set the letter aside, her heart skipping as her mind whirled with possibilities.

Did Eliza have a lover she left behind?

Had she been brought to England to remove her from George and then been made to marry Lord Leyac?

By all accounts she had loved Lord Leyac, but had she really, or had she just been good at playing at it out of duty?

She opened the next letter,

My dearest Eliza,

I must admit to being rather miffed at your letter and your constant refusal to come home, I know you are worried at the reaction your father might have at your defiance of him, but you can let me handle that problem. Oh do cooperate and come home! You know fine well I didn't want you to go in the first place, it's all nonsense about finding a husband. And I recall that you didn't want to go to England to find a husband yourself anyway, but now you have the perfect opportunity to come home and you still refuse. I know your sense of duty appalls at the idea of such defiance, but my dear, let me handle all that. I miss you, please come home. We can go away, anywhere, America perhaps?"

your loving and dearest George.

Anna closed the letter and flicked through the pile she was holding, they all appeared in the same hand. She stared at them thoughtfully. Eliza had a lover? Maybe, Catherine's anger and resentment towards Eliza, and subsequently Anna's mother, Elizabeth, was because of this. Anna stood up taking the letters with her, she needed to think. She tied the bow again and picked up a few other items she thought looked interesting, a notebook, a small ornamental bird and a soft silk scarf.

She stowed the items in her room and went to bed falling into a fitful restless sleep, tossing and turning through the night.

CHAPTER THIRTEEN

Anna

After her restless night, Anna felt a morning walk in the fresh air might do her some good, and simply getting out of the stifling air and confusion she felt surrounding this place was an urge she couldn't ignore.

She left by the back hall passageway, pausing only to grab the letter addressed to her in Olivia's handwriting from the front hall table. Pulling on a pair of wellingtons and an overcoat hanging by the back doorway, which looked too plain and unstylish to be Flynn's, she thought, as she went down the little steps, remembering the diary description of her mother hiding here the night she left, and crunched her wellingtons along the gravel.

The boots and coat probably belonged to her brother and she wondered whether they were both the same size, although the boots were a little on the big side.

She moved away from the house and out of the gates that marked the exit to the gardens, and out into the fields beyond. She didn't have any idea where she was going and part of her was screaming at herself for doing the one thing she hated - being out in the wind and drizzle tramping round muddy places, but she felt somehow today, that this is exactly what she needed, and just getting some clear space between herself and everything was best.

Maybe it was because getting outside was exactly what her mother would have done. But, despite her dislike of the country, even she had to admit she really was breathing easier out here, surrounded by nothing, with no one to judge, ask questions, or trying to manipulate her - she just walked her troubles away.

She paused by a solitary bench and sat watching the morning sun skimming the hillside in the distance. Opening Olivia's letter, she began to read:

My dearest Anna,

I have been simply desperate for news from you for an age.

Anyway, I am writing to let you know that I am coming to stay. And there is no use arguing, it is all arranged. I am taking a leave of absence from the Hospital, well it is an enforced leave if you must know but I will send a telegram with details shortly. I am greatly looking forward to my adventure in the north. I have never travelled so far before.

I am perfectly aware you would never ask me to come, or even admit you needed help, but I know you will be in need of a friendly face, so there's no use arguing. And besides, it's not everyday your friend inherits an estate and the title 'Lady'.

I know you don't plan to keep the estate, but I'm coming anyway to make sure that nasty Flynn doesn't do anything else terrible.

I'm making arrangements this end and shall be in touch with details of my travel arrangements shortly.

Yours,

Olivia,

Anna folded the letter frowning, Olivia really was far too impulsive but she had to admit it would be nice to have her here and she was a little worried why Olivia had been put on enforced leave from the hospital. Something must have happened for that to have been forced on her. Something terrible.

She thought back to the last time she'd seen Olivia. She had been tired and now Anna thought about it, the dark circles under her eyes were more pronounced than usual, but Anna had thought that was just the constant bombing, combined with long shifts in the hospital, but what if it was more than that?

Anna, pushed the thoughts aside and decided to make her tell what was going on. She hoped it wasn't just a case of Anna being too wrapped up in her own problems to notice.

She glanced up at the sun again and wandered further, thinking about Olivia.

There would also be the awkward conversation about her beau being the same Johnson who was with her brother when he'd died and the only one who knew what happened.

But she wasn't likely to find that out anytime soon with him locked in a POW camp.

So deep in thought she barely realised where she was going when she found herself tramping towards a large one storey farmhouse with a half stone wall and courtyard out the front. To her right in the distance she could see a group of land-girls.

She moved towards the courtyard thinking the farmhouse was very different from that of Sissy Jenkins's family.

She must go see Margaret Jenkins and tell her she had been right all along, her sister had never stolen the child. Anna found that kind of belief fascinating, even when all evidence appeared against them.

She pushed the thought to the back of her mind's to-do list as a middle aged man wearing a woollen sleeveless cardigan and shirt with rolled up sleeves and trousers tucked into muddy Wellington boots approached her.

"You're Miss Anna, from the big house," he said stating it as if she didn't know her own name.

"Yes," she said stunned. It was still a bit of a jolt when people recognised her and it threw her off for a moment, so she just stood there for a few seconds wondering what to say.

"Come in Miss, we're so glad you've finally been found and can now get stuck into running the place properly. I mean I had a great respect for your brother, but that place was never meant to be a museum. Oh listen to me rambling away and not even introducing myself. My name is Gerald and I have been the tenant farmer here since my father died leaving it to me."

"Pleased to meet you."

"Your brother used to come down regular like to speak to us about how things were going, I'm glad you're going to do the same. I don't mind saying, we've missed him. And that Flynn..." he paused. "...well never mind anyway. Come. Come inside the wife is baking a fresh batch of scones."

"Thank you." Anna replied weakly after his retreating back as he moved towards the door to the farmhouse. With little else to do, and feeling a refusal would be rude, she followed and stood hesitantly in the doorway.

"Mrs," he called, "you won't believe who has come to visit."

A large bosomed woman with a round face and frizzy curls poked her head around the doorway to the hall where Anna and Gerald were now stood. Anna watched Gerald struggling to pull off his boots and wondered if she should offer to help.

The woman had flour smudges on her face and her apron was covered in splashes of white dough, her hands all floury and white.

"Oh!" she said, "hello there,"

"This my dear," he said yanking off the last boot with a big heave, "is Miss Leyac, from the house, come to visit us. I recognised her straight away, she's a look of her mother and her mannerisms are Thomas all over, you can tell they're twins can't you my dear?" he said looking over at Anna with an approving smile.

The woman smiled and disappeared back round the doorway, calling from within,

"Come in, I'll make us some tea," and began clattering, which Anna presumed was her putting the kettle on the stove.

Anna followed Gerald into a large warm kitchen with a delicious smell of fresh bread and scones all mixed together. Anna sniffed appreciatively, her stomach growling. The warmth of the room wrapped around her dispersed the coldness of outside, like a warm comforting blanket.

"Sit, sit my dear, I'll make us some tea while Gerald gets the paperwork ready," she waved one floury hand mid air towards a series of chairs surrounding the large wooden table.

Anna chose a chair and sat watching the woman wipe her hands on a tea towel and quickly move to set out cups and saucers.

"Really there's no need to fuss, I didn't mean to intrude, let me go and leave you to get on with your baking Mrs…"

"Please, call me Martha, and don't you move, I won't hear of it. I'll be heartily offended if you leave without having a cup of tea and sampling a scone." The woman smiled at her.

Anna returned the smile and sat back in the chair while Martha poured tea from the pot.

Anna began to feel more relaxed than she had in ages.

Gerald, who had disappeared through a connecting door in the far side of the room, returned as Martha finished pouring the tea.

His arms were laden with large books and a ledger, which he placed in front of Anna with a smile of pride before sitting down at the corner of the table and taking a sip of the tea Martha had already poured for him.

"You'll see that everything is there," he said.

"I don't understand," she said confused

He leaned forward and opened the ledger on the top of the pile. Neat columns of figures lined each page.

"I'm sorry I think you're confused."

"You are Miss Leyac?"

"Yes, but…"

"Well then, here you go. Here's the farm accounts and receipts of everything. You've come to check how we're doing?"

"No I haven't," she said closing the ledger.

Both Gerald and Martha stared at her confused.

"But as master, or should I say mistress, of Leyac estate it's your job to ensure all the tenants are performing, your brother used to come regular like, I am proud of my accounts," Gerald smiled.

"He's meticulous with them," Martha said. "Gerald I think maybe we've jumped in too quickly in our happiness that a true Leyac is now in charge, she probably just wanted to meet us today, and come another time to see the accounts."

"Of course," Gerald slapped his hand against his head, "I'm sorry, we can do this on your next visit, let me get these out of your way. I'm sorry again Miss."

"You've both misunderstood. I've not come here for either of the reasons you think." They both stopped and looked at her curiously. "If truth is told, I came here by mistake, I had no idea you were a tenant farmer for the Leyac estate. I was simply out for a walk this morning when I came across your farm."

"Ah. Well at least now you know where we are, you'll know where to come when you do want to check the accounts. How often do you want to come? Once every three months?"

"No, that won't be possible. You see, I'm not keeping the estate. I'm signing it over to Flynn."

They both stared at her in stunned silence, mouths slightly open in disbelief, a cold hostility entering the room then as the awkward silence continued.

"Why would you do such a monstrous thing?" Martha asked shock and disbelief evident in her tone.

"Monstrous? I hardly think that's fair." Anna said, a note of indigance in her voice.

"We don't understand why you would give over something so important to such a person."

"Because he is already running the place, he knows what he's doing. He also has the means and money to do it. I am just a journalist from London, I know nothing about running an estate, and I really don't want to be in charge of a museum about my life - a life I've had no part of and, until a few weeks ago, had no idea existed."

"He's only running the place because he spent his life leeching off Lord Leyac, worming his way to the top, that doesn't mean he's any good for the place, and it doesn't mean he knows what he's doing. He does what's best for himself, he doesn't care what happens to the place as long as it's bringing him the money he needs. And if you don't want the museum, change it. Do something else with it, do something for the war effort. I heard about a place in Scotland being used as a school, what about something like that?" said Gerald.

"How could I do that, I'm a journalist."

"You're a Leyac, and the only living one at that. You owe it to your family to take back what is yours. It's your money and your estate," said Martha

"I don't want it. I just want my life the way it was. I want to go back to being a journalist."

"But you could do so much good with what you have been handed, you could really help the war, you could really make a difference in people's lives in a way you can't by just going back to London," said Martha.

"It's just not for me, I can't run a place like that alone."

"We have a son, Martha and me, he's 20 and ripe for military service. He desperately wants to go fight but, he can't because he's a farmer, and it's protected. He can't go and do what he wants, he knows he's needed here and he's accepted it. He just gets on with the job because it's his duty. This, my dear, is your duty. Your duty is to your country and what you could do with the power the Leyac name and money can give you. You owe it to the memory of your mother, your poor dead brother who wasted his whole life looking for you, and to your dear dead father who died at sea in the Great War."

"I'm sorry," she said standing, "but it's just not what I want," she moved to leave.

"Then if you only do what you want, that makes you no better than Flynn himself. I hope you are happy in London, and when this war is over and the estate is bankrupt because Flynn has squeezed everything from it, you can look back and not regret your decision. Good day Miss Leyac," Gerald stood and left the room, Martha looked at her sadly.

"You must excuse my husband, he and your brother were very close, he thought of him like a son, and he still finds his death hard. I understand your decision but what he said was right, you really must carefully consider your position my dear. Don't be too quick to give away what you don't know you have."

Anna nodded and left the way she had come, her mind whirling.

What did he know of her and her family?

How dare he say she's just as bad as Flynn.

Damn him!

She was nothing like Flynn, what was so wrong with just wanting her life back?

Anna tramped back the way she had come, the cold wind biting at her face as she walked. The coldness wrapping itself around her and infecting her lungs with a sharp bitterness. She really did hate the damn countryside.

Sorry mother, it's just not me, she said looking up to the swirling grey clouds above.

How could they possibly know anything about her, or why she was making the decision she was? And to compare her with that snake Flynn. She was nothing like him. Why was it so wrong to want things to just go back to the way they were before all this mess began.

She didn't ask to be given this responsibility and if she had left it all alone and not got herself embroiled in the whole investigation into Elizabeth Leyac in the first place, no one would have been any the wiser.

She was angry at them, but more angry at herself and her own stubborn curiosity, without which none of this would have happened.

She stomped back towards the looming house, hating the cold, wind and damn countryside even more. Damn it, damn it all. Why did things have to be so difficult?

The sharp biting words played over and again in her head, "you're no better than Flynn…"

Bloody fools, they've lived so long in their insular world they knew nothing of anything else.

How the hell did they expect her to take charge of an estate?

How would you even begin to do such a thing?

Idiots.

They knew nothing.

What made them think she would be better at it than Flynn?

She might even be worse. She seemed to be good at making a mess of things.

As she reached the steps to the side entrance, she ran up just as she felt spots of rain. Flinging open the heavy door and entering she flung the boots and coat where she had found them and moved back towards the main hall and stairway. Her face set with anger.

She was going to get this sorted once and for all and she was going to do it now.

CHAPTER FOURTEEN

Anna

As she passed through to the main square hallway and alongside the entrance to the dining room, heading towards the staircase, she heard her name called.

"Ah there you are Anna, I have been looking for you," Flynn's all too sweet tone changed to a note of reproach.

She stopped, fists in balls.

"Come my dear, sit and take tea, I have the paperwork prepared, and I have taken the liberty of calling on your council. Mr. Blackwood will be arriving presently. In fact, is that the car I hear now… come my dear, I do dislike conversing through a wall, it is most inconvenient."

Anna moved towards the dining room feeling a little less angry that finally things were getting sorted out. This really was it now. The time had come for him to show his hand and she had no doubt it would have a biting sting for her, but what and how?

Frankly she didn't care so long as she could go home and pick up the pieces of her life.

Flynn was sat at the head of the table, quietly eating a boiled egg, and for a moment, anger forgotten, she watched him, her mouth watering at the idea of such coveted food, the like of which were more than scarce in London. Well, he may have eggs and all kinds of food we don't have in London, but he doesn't have the spirit of a Londoner, the sense of survival, she thought to herself.

Gerald's words rang in her head, "you're no better than Flynn" it said as she watched him scoop out his egg calmly, as if nothing at all were out the ordinary.

"Please sit, my dear, do you wish for an egg?" he said.

"Yes, thank you that would be lovely," she said genuinely.

He continued without looking up but spoke aloud as if speaking to his food, "Fetch another egg."

A young girl left the room following this order, Anna watched her leave then glanced back at Flynn.

Anna sat, pouring herself tea from the fine china teapot into the vacant cup near her plate watching Flynn not meet her gaze. His manner and confidence was someone perfectly at home in his surroundings, an air of commanding authority exuding from him. Despite this she remained fascinated with his graceful movements and his calm blank expression. Even the eyes, dark pools Anna couldn't read - he was a closed book and Anna was curious as to what was beneath the exterior.

"Now my dear Miss Forrester," he said putting down his spoon and reaching for his cup. "Today we will sort out this little bump in the road. Mr. Blackwood and my own counsel will arrive shortly and we will go through the paperwork and the steps required of you."

"Required?" Anna said, her heart beginning to hammer.

"All in good time, look here is your egg. Eat Miss Forrester, so we can get on with things," he said as the girl re-entered the room.

The girl had an egg perfectly balanced inside a small china egg cup. She set it down, curtsied and moved away.

Anna savored every mouthful and was sure eggs before the war had never tasted so good.

However, she was acutely aware of the strained silence between herself and Flynn. He appeared perfectly happy and relaxed.

Was he really just pleased to be getting rid of her?

Yes, you're giving him everything he wants a voice told her.

But, what did it matter if it meant she could go back to her life in London.

What concern of hers was it of what he did in this house?

Or Gerald and the other tenants?

They were nothing to do with her, Gerald was wrong in that.

She thought again of the portrait of Eliza hidden away in the loft for years, her mother's room and how it exhaled her essence from every corner, the lonely grave of the apparent Elizabeth, but which in fact had contained poor Sissy.

Flynn rose from the table and went to ring the long corded rope bell on the wall, bringing her back from her thoughts. She scraped an imaginary sliver of egg from her plate.

"Come Miss Forrester," he said holding the back of her chair to pull it out for her.

She rose just as the elderly butler came into the room.

"Ah, could you show our visitors upstairs to the drawing room when they arrive, Miss Forrester and I will await them there. And, send up tea and coffee," Flynn ordered moving towards the door.

The butler nodded and left.

Flynn left the room and Anna followed, as if behind a school teacher, up the stairs past the portraits and into the drawing room, where he sat himself upright in a chair nearest the fireplace, which was crackling and popping away. He began tapping his foot.

Her anger rose and threatened to bubble over, but she suppressed it and moved towards the window looking down onto the circular driveway surrounding the central grass area, and the statue marking its centre. She hated most of all Flynn's attitude of entitlement, as if she were lesser than he, but if she chose, she could take over the estate and put him in his place. She smiled a little at the thought of being the one holding the power for once.

As she watched, she heard him clear his throat, and she looked at the reflection of his outline in the window pane, before her attention again focused on the outside as a car slowly turned into the circular driveway, fine rain splattering from the roof.

The car came to a stop at the entrance steps and two men got out, one she recognised as Mr. Blackwood, the other was a small ferrety man, slightly hunched over. Both held briefcases and mounted the steps, disappearing into the house below.

Some minutes later both men were shown into the room. Anna, still by the window, watched. Flynn went over and shook hands with the small ferrety man, whose eyes darted around the room. He had a shifty expression that made Anna wary.

"This is Miss Forrester," Flynn introduced her and she took his hand, which was cool and clammy. She shuddered as his eyes darted all over her, narrowing.

Edward Blackwood moved beside Anna and Flynn set himself back in his chair by the fireplace.

"Come everyone, let's get on with business. There's no need for formalities. I believe you have the paperwork ready?" Flynn turned to the ferrety man who nodded and sat by Flynn opening his briefcase.

"Yes indeed Mr. Flynn, I have everything here," his voice was nasally and had a subtle whine note to it.

He removed a stack of paperwork from his briefcase and held them aloft, Edward Blackwood moved to take them from him and shifted to begin reading them in a corner chair by Anna.

The room fell silent, Anna turned to the window again and instead of looking out, ran her hand along the rough wooden window frame and the wobbly panes, made long ago, feeling the cold dampness of the glass and the rough bumps of the wood.

"I think you will find everything is in order,." Flynn's voice held a note of irritation, he quickly masked.

"I am sure you are right, but I must read the terms and conditions, for my client's sake, otherwise I would be doing her a disservice."

There was a disgruntled humph from the corner.

"Miss Forrester," Edward said, "are you quite clear on the terms regarding Scotland? You didn't mention it to me," his voice had a slight hint of reproach.

"What about Scotland? I know nothing of this."

"Ah," the nasally voice interjected, "that is a requirement of the contract. Miss Forrester must remove herself to Scotland, it is all arranged, we have set up a place to live, an allowance and everything is ready for her to go there, I have taken the liberty of giving notice to your landlady in London and have arranged for your things to be moved there directly. There is nothing left for you to do, I have made the whole thing as painless as possible. All you need to do is sign. If you turn to page six, Mr. Blackwood…"

"What? Scotland? I can't go to Scotland, I am going back to London. I'm a journalist I need to be in London for my career. I'm sorry for your trouble, but what made you think I would ever go to Scotland?"

"You misunderstand Miss Forrester, Scotland is a requirement of the contract, it is not negotiable." The nasally whine was becoming irritating.

"You cannot tell me where I can and can't live. Once I sign this damn house over to Flynn, I am free to do as I please," she said her voice rising.

"Unfortunately Miss Forrester that is not the case. You are a Leyac by birth and although you are signing over everything to Mr. Flynn, you will still remain under the Leyac estate and receive an allowance for the purpose of your living expenses. Continuing as a journalist is out of the question. You need to remain as anonymous as possible, and that means doing as the estate and the contract requires," he continued in his whiny drone.

"Edward, can they do this?"

"Once you sign this contract, you are signing that you agree to this. So yes they can. But I must..."

"Never mind any of that, don't you just want to get rid of the place. Just sign it and we'll work out the details later," Flynn said.

"No I bloody well won't just sign it, until you say this Scotland thing is nonsense."

Flynn jumped to his feet anger in his eyes. Anna watched as he tried to control the emotions on his usually composed face, beads of sweat on his perfectly smooth forehead.

Edward Blackwood cleared his throat, "Might I have a few moments with my client."

Flynn opened his mouth to speak, then looked over at Blackwood before sighing.

"Yes, my counsel and I will await you in the library, but I urge you Miss Forrester, do not trifle with me." He got up and stalked off.

He left with the ferrety man scurrying after him, clutching his paperwork, eyes darting from Anna to Blackwood all the time.

* * *

"I would strongly advise you not to sign this Miss Forrester."

"Why is that?"

"Well for one I would like to study this contract before you sign it, and I suspect Flynn won't want that to happen. I fear he is trying to tie you into a legal contract that will be very hard for you to break."

"Is it right what he says, essentially I have to do what he says."

"Yes, from what I can gather it essentially means that you are under obligation to do as the estate wishes, which in terms of this contract means moving to Scotland. I urge you Miss Forrester, do not indebt yourself to Flynn like this. I can see he is not someone to take defeat easily but if you sign this, you will never have a life that is your own. You will be beholden to him and this estate for the rest of your life."

"It seems Mr. Blackwood, that no matter what I choose, I am under obligation to this estate in one way or another. I can see now why my mother accepted the fate of her allowance and chose to keep her identity a secret. I am learning rapidly that no matter what I do, this estate and the legacy of the Leyac name has a reach so vast, it's like roots growing deep beneath the earth, so that before you realise, it has invaded and taken over your life. I wonder if my life was ever my own." Anna paused, surveying the room, the crackling of the fire popping, "Get them in here, let's end this shall we Mr. Blackwood."

When they were again seated, Anna looked at each of them in turn,

"It seems that I must accept certain truths and conditions of my life now."

Flynn nodded a faint hint of approval as a flicker of relief creased his expression.

"It would seem," Anna continued, "that in order to be free of the constraints of the Leyac estate and its ties I must give up my life in London and go to Scotland. However, this in itself isn't free at all. So I must either accept that this is how my life is now, or," she paused.

Flynn sat forward in his chair.

"I keep the estate."

The ferrety man looked up sharply from his paperwork.

Flynn on his feet now, "How ridiculous. Surely that's not what you want."

"What I want doesn't matter. You made that perfectly clear. I have decided to keep the estate and take up my rightful place as heir."

"You can't do that." Flynn blustered in an octave higher than usual, then began pacing.

"Ah, I interject Mr. Flynn she can indeed," the ferrety man interrupted.

"Oh do be quiet, you are supposed to help me, not her."

"I serve the estate not you Mr. Flynn."

"I see how it is, you turncoat. Well you're fired."

"On the contrary, if Miss Leyac is keeping the estate, she is the one with the power to fire me."

"What game are you playing Forrester?"

"No game. You have my decision."

"Don't be a fool."

She shrugged and he turned away stalking off.

"Flynn," she called him back. He turned, "you're fired."

"You can't do that."

"On the contrary, yes I can. Your biggest mistake was to take everything from me. London was all I had left and by taking that, you left me with nothing to lose. And someone with nothing to lose, has nothing left to fear."

"You don't know how to run an estate."

"True."

"You need me."

"No I don't think I do. Get your things, and get out of my

house."

"Damn you to hell," he stomped off, rage all over his usually calm facade, "I won't let this happen."

She turned to the ferrety man. "You can take Mr. Blackwood through all aspects of the legal paperwork and such like. I want him to be privy to everything related to the estate and Flynn's deals," he nodded.

"Can I just congratulate you Miss Leayc…"

"No you may not, just do as I instruct. Mr. Blackwood is now in charge, I expect you to give him what he requires. You may leave and go prepare the necessary files and paperwork for Mr. Blackwood."

He got up and scurried out the room.

She turned to Blackwood. He was smiling up at her, "Well done," he said.

She ignored the comment. "Watch that man. I don't trust him," she said watching the ferrety man scurry down the steps of the driveway below.

"Oh I will don't worry, Miss. I will leave you now, there is much work to be done."

"Can you look into the financial state of the estate for me, I need to know what I'm dealing with."

"It's already on my list of things to look into."

He bowed and left the room.

Anna turned back to the window. A sense of dread and relief washing over her at once.

What on earth had she just done?

She moved around the room feeling the fabric of the chairs, and moved out towards the round gallery staring up at the portraits of her family.

She noticed then the portrait of her brother had the hint of a smile, hiding much of himself but promising something more.

Just like mother's.

She wondered why she'd never noticed it before.

As she looked up studying the curve of his jawline, the sweep of his hair and the determined privilege behind the eyes, she wondered how much of their father was in him. How much was in her?

Well, I've done it now, she silently told the portrait. What a fool I am.

CHAPTER FIFTEEN

Prisoner

Johnson woke in the darkness, sweat dripping from him despite the cold air of the room and the chill of the wind blowing through the gaps in the door.

He gasped catching his breath, he had that dream again, the one about the boy who got himself shot, but this time he had been in his plane on the day it crash landed. In the dream he had poured fuel all over the plane interior and set it alight then realised the boy was there and he had burned him alive, then Schmidt held him back as he tried to save the boy, laughing as he held on tight while the boy screamed in pain. Schmidt's cold, cruel laughter echoing in unison with the boy's screams.

Johnson shook his head, to disperse the ugly dream, he really needed to pull himself together. He'd got out of solitary after another grueling week with Schmidt for company. Captain Smith had been furious with what he'd done, said he'd compromised the committee and their plans.

Sitting up and putting his head in his hands he tried to force the dream images of the boy from his head. He rubbed his eyes, the dampness of his hot sweat now turning cool and making him shiver in the cold morning.

He massaged his tender ribs. That Schmidt had a knack of knowing just where to hurt.

He glanced towards the window, the cold frost outside clung to the hut windows and Johnson could see his breath before him.

Jumping down from his bunk, his boots thudded and he stamped them to warm up his feet as he moved towards the central burner, burning low warmth, the others surrounding it, clutching tin mugs of watery tea.

Johnson did the same, noting to himself how much like cattle they were, huddling like herded animals in this place.

The dire routine of waking, surviving, eating just enough, and waiting.

Waiting for what?

Waiting to live?

Waiting to die?

Johnson felt sure the end of the war was a long way off yet, despite what the others said. He couldn't decide whether he felt happy to be alive, or sad to be alive in this place.

The only thing he was sure of was that he was sick and tired of being confined, dictated to and treated like cattle. He touched his ribs again, and those dammed dreams were driving him mad.

Why he couldn't just forget the boy and his stupid sacrifice?

A sacrifice for the sake of what?

Some ridiculous idea of an ill-thought out escape plan.

What was he thinking?

Did he actually think he could escape?

Right there in front of everyone. Was he really that naive?

He just couldn't understand why the boy had done it.

A voice in the back of his head reminded him of his own ill-conceived escape and he ignored it.

That had simply been bad luck.

He clutched his tin mug tightly, his fingers going white as he clenched the hot mug between his cold hands as thoughts tumbled one after another, so he felt almost alone in the hut, alone with nothing but his thoughts torturing him.

The day of his plane crash, the poor sod burning - even though he already knew the man was dead when the fire began, but this didn't stop him feeling as if the poor chap had burned needlessly.

But now with this stupid boy killing himself trying to escape over the fence during roll-call, all Johnson could see was their faces alive right before it happened.

The smell of the boy's blood seemed to be everywhere.

"Hey, Johnson, you all right? You don't look so good?"

He snapped out of his trance.

"Of course,' he replied giving Andrews a smile of resignation, or was it one of unfathomable hidden thoughts? He certainly had hidden thoughts, lots of them, and he could see everyone else around him was feeling the same.

But there in that moment he could almost see the hint of understanding in his fellow prisoner.

Andrews, came from some unheard of place down in the depths of the west country, very beautiful by all accounts, and the lilt of his warm west country accent reminded Johnson of visits down that way as a boy. An oddly warm comforting accent that in quieter times Johnson might have ribbed him for.

Andrews was a strong muscular sort of chap, the kind that wasn't that way from physical activity, although he was no doubt very fit, but was naturally strong and lean, his upbringing on a farm no-doubt adding to his already natural strength before he joined the forces.

Looking over at Andrews now as he clutched his mug between large rough hands, Johnson wondered why, with such good natural strength, he had joined the RAF and not the Army. His physicality would certainly have been an asset.

He opened his mouth to ask this when the alarm sounded for roll call.

They filed out in a rough herded line and the cold sharp, dry air bit at his lungs as he breathed.

His eyes moved to the spot where the young boy had been killed and he was sure the blood and smell of death still infected his eyes and his nostrils, or was he imagining it?

The spot was clean, as if nothing had ever taken place, as if the whole thing had been simply and clearly tidied away in a very neat and orderly fashion.

He was nudged in the ribs and jumped at the pain. As he looked around he heard his name called. He quickly replied with a short sharp assignation of his presence.

Johnson returned to his bunk and laid back crossing his booted feet and smoking - blowing the smoke into the air. He would have to watch his cigarette supply and maybe ration himself more, but right now he just didn't damn well care.

He drowned out the noise of the room, the chatter of his fellow prisoners, the sound of a game of cards, others in a far corner practising their language lessons, the sounds of the broken syllables crossing the air like snapshots of disjointed conversations.

He ignored the scratch of those writing letters, the flip, flip of cards, the foreign words, and let them fade to a distant drone, as he let himself sink into a quiet depressed frustration at his situation.

His thoughts were interrupted by a shout from the other side that new prisoners were being herded in from the main gate.

He looked up interested and jumped down from his bunk to follow the curious crowd in the doorway.

A fairly small group of airmen were being herded in and pushed into various huts.

His heart began to hammer and a tingling sensation of shock and disbelief ran though his body as he stared at just one of those prisoners.

This one, he thought with dread, could be a problem and he stubbed out the last of his cigarette.

As the group got closer he could see his gaze was met equally by one of familiarity and the two stared in recognition at each other.

Johnson swore under his breath.

The Nazi pushed two towards a hut opposite and the final two including the one Johnson recognised, towards his own hut.

They all made way for the new men and Captain Smith introduced himself, shaking hands with both of them. He then introduced each of the men in the hut. All were all keen for news of home asking multiple questions at once.

Smith interjected and told everyone to be quiet.

Silence fell and they all watched as the two new boys patiently shook hands and said a greeting to each man.

When it was his turn, he held his breath as Captain Smith said, "Lieutenant Johnson, a keen footballer who will trade anything for another pack of smokes.

He put on a fake smile and held out his hand.

The newcomer just stared at him through shrewd eyes, and said, "will he now, Captain Smith? Well that is interesting,"

As they moved to the next man, Johnson watched his retreating back.

Something had to be done and fast, but what?

He needed to think. This was a problem, a big one, for here was a man who knew things, and he didn't understand the danger he'd be creating if he revealed them.

This one could blow everything.

He must speak to him quickly, before he gave him up and made things worse.

But what could he say?

Damn this was not ideal, not in the least.

Later, laid on his bunk reading his latest letter from Olivia, he frowned slightly as she told how she had helped a young boy who had to have his leg amputated.

"Poor kid," he mused as he read on taking a drag on the last of his cigarette.

She moved on to talk about her friend.

One of the older men shouted across the room waving his own letter, "Hey men, listen to this.."

The whole hut stopped reading and looked up with distracted interest.

"My missus," he said, "says that London's had bombers raiding every single night since September. Can you believe that? They'll be nowt left of London, bloody Nazi bastards."

The newcomer, moved towards the door, unnoticed by all except Johnson and looked pointedly at him to make it clear he wanted him to follow.

He slipped down from his bunk, and quietly followed, while the rest of the room were still listening to the letter from 'the misuses' about London's air raids.

Johnson's growing sense of dread made him fidget with the edges of his own letter, still clutched between his fingers.

As he followed the newcomer down the steps of the hut to the frozen ground below, he blew out an icy breath as he stopped beside him, both watching ahead. The newcomer handed him a cigarette and they stood in silence for a moment as Johnson lit it and inhaled deeply.

"So…" he said, the tone in his voice poignant.

Johnson sighed, taking another drag on his cigarette, "Look, things are complicated."

"Really? How complicated that you need to hold back from your fellow countrymen? If I didn't know better I'd say that's suspicious. I never would have pegged you for a traitor."

Johnson lowered his voice, "You've got the wrong end of it. I'm not a Nazi spy, There are things I must keep secret for the sake of national security."

"Really?" The newcomer adopted an unconvinced tone.

"Yes, if the Nazi's knew the information I have we'd all be done for. I can't risk them finding out."

"So are you a spy for our lot then?"

"Let's just say our school German lessons came in handy."

The newcomer laughed, "You always were top in languages."

"Well you must promise you'll keep quiet. It's absolutely vital."

"To the Nazi's? You don't need to worry about that. But to our lot, I can't promise."

"Damn you. You could ruin everything. You must keep your mouth shut."

The newcomer shrugged, finished his cigarette, blew out the last of his smoke and walked away back into the hut without another word.

Johnson swore to himself. This was a problem, a real problem.

How was he going to deal with this?

He'd have to talk to Smith, he needed to be bumped up the queue for escape attempts. If they found out he'd been withholding information, they would make life difficult in here.

He finished the last of his cigarette and moved back into the hut.

Damn it, he thought to himself this was a complication he didn't need.

His escape would have to happen in the next few days, and come what may.

Olivia sprung to mind and he knew he shouldn't have got involved with her, but he couldn't help it, she was the only link with Blighty he had at the moment.

He went back into the hut, the newcomer now back in his own bunk watching Jones, who had taken over from the other man and was now reading his letter.

The room roared as Jones' wife mentioned she had seen some women going out without stockings.

He looked over, his interest piqued momentarily, then returned to his own letter, smoothing out the creases he'd worried into it.

But try as he might, he couldn't stop the ringing in his ears as his heart boomed away and the words blurred as his mind wandered. He glanced towards Smith and knew he must think of a way to get him to bump-up his escape attempt.

Damn the Nazis. Damn this war.

He glanced over at the newcomer and locked eyes with him.

Johnson glanced away.

Seeing Smith leaving the hut he jumped down from his bunk and followed with a quick backwards glance at the newcomer still watching him.

Outside he moved his hands under his arms to keep warm and jogged to catch Smith.

"Sir?"

Smith turned, "Johnson. What can I do for you?" he said continuing to walk.

"Sir, I know it's a big ask, but I need to be bumped to the top of the escape list."

Smith stopped and faced him.

"Why?"

"It's really important I get home."

"Why?"

Johnson sighed, "It just is. Can you take my word for it?"

"No I can't. You've already betrayed the committee trying that fool-hardy attempt that got you in solitary. You refused then to tell me what was going on and now you want me to go against my men, the committee and those who've waited patiently for their turn, to let you go first and for no good reason. I'm sorry Johnson, it's not happening."

He turned and started walking again.

"Sir, please."

He stopped again a little way ahead.

"Are you going to tell me what's going on and what you're keeping back?"

Johnson was silent.

"I thought not," Smith said and walked away.

"Bloody hell!" He swore and kicked a stone. "Now what?" he said to the sky.

The clouds gave the sky a white-grey and heavy look, the air icy. It felt like snow was on the way.

Not the best time of year to escape, but needs must. He would have to go alone after all, but this time with a better plan than the last one.

He walked the perimeter of the camp re-examining it's weak points and concluded the best bet was still the back fence closest to the woods.

Moving back to the hut for warmth, he stepped in and rubbed his hands together by the central stove.

Glancing up he saw the newcomer talking to Smith in his office.

Damn it!

That's it then, he would have to go tonight.

He looked out the window as the first flakes of snow began to fall.

CHAPTER SIXTEEN

Anna

Reeling from her ridiculously impulsive decision, her mind was whirling with the enormity of what she had done.

What a damned fool.

She paced back and forth by the window seat in the long gallery. It had been stubbornness and injustice but why, oh why, did she always choose the difficult path?

Her mind wandered to the letter she had received from the old housekeeper telling of the day Lady Catherine, on becoming mistress of the Leyac estate, had sacked the entire staff right where she stood now. The ghosts of what had occurred then whirled around her like a wind, pressing oppressively on her skull, as the feeling of dread in her stomach grew.

She had no idea what to do now.

She glanced out of the window; the trees that led away from the estate and down towards the village snaked out in front of the entrance gate and she watched them blowing in the cold breeze, their branches waving in a frenzy of tangled bare spindles. The day was grey and cold, much like her mood.

Damn Flynn. Why couldn't he have just let her go back to London?

Still, she must do something, so she turned towards the staircase more purposefully than she felt, and marched towards the door that led to the staff staircase and basement.

She slowed as she reached the twisting steep steps and heard low voices murmuring. She didn't pause in case her nerve failed her, but she wanted to.

Pushing open the door to the large room filled with people, they stopped their chatter abruptly and stared at her.

Anna cleared her throat, "I thought you should all be the first to know, I am staying on permanently."

There was silence in the room for a few moments and Anna, feeling awkward, started to leave.

"Miss," a small female voice interrupted stopping her, "will you be keeping things as they are or making changes?"

"I don't know yet, what will be happening, but I can say I will let you know. Oh and I should mention. Mr Julien Flynn has been fired."

"Is that a wise decision, Ma'am?" The elderly butler asked, "with all respect, what do you know of running an estate and museum?"

"I understand your concern but I was hoping you would all help me out, and the museum will remain closed."

This time she didn't hesitate and turned to leave, pulling her frame upright to leave no room for any further doubt.

How could she tell them all she had no idea what she was doing? That the sudden decision in anger seemed foolish now? And, seeing their faces, the faces of real people who now depended on her made her feel sick to her stomach.

How could she possibly tell any of them that.

She really must learn fast, and get better - much better. Calming her breathing on the way back up the stairs, she considered all the possible people she could ask to help her.

In the green room she found the place in disarray, papers, folders, books and receipts were piled up in the room in various haphazard ways.

She moved the stacks of papers to a corner of floor space and dropped them with a thud. Flynn had been through here in a hurry she thought, wondering what he'd taken and how he would use it.

She began pulling open the desk drawers and rooting through looking, but she wasn't sure what for. How could she know if things had gone missing but it felt better to at least try. It was then she saw the stack of photographs in the back corner of the middle drawer.

She pulled them out and examined the face, it was her brother. He was young, maybe about 17 and was riding a bike down a big hill with his legs outstretched to the side, so the bicycle coasted down the hill, his face alight with laughter and mischief.

The next was a photo of him laid on his back, the wide brimmed hat of his school uniform just covering the top of his face, arms clasped behind his head and legs crossed at the feet. The photo looked like it had been taken by the side of some kind of river or lake in the summer.

Another photograph was taken here on the estate, in cold weather, her brother, younger this time, wrapped up in a big overcoat and scarf. In one hand he had a large stick and a large shaggy dog alongside him had his eyes firmly fixed on the stick.

She flicked through the rest, they were all of her brother.

Seeing photos of him made her feel like she was seeing a little of his personality; he seemed like he'd been fun-loving, if these were anything to go by.

Here was a whole life she had never known, had never been a part of, and which he had spent endlessly looking for her, until this war killed him, like so many others.

She put the photographs back, her eyes resting on the telephone and without thinking picked it up.

The crackling sound and clicks as the line was connected seemed to take ages but then it began to ring.

A young female voice answered, "Hello, Doctor Laker's office, how can I help?"

The words stuck. What would she even say?

"Hello…" the girl said again.

Anna said nothing.

"Hello is anyone there?"

She hung up her breath coming fast.

What was she thinking?

She couldn't speak to him.

He had said that had been it. And she didn't want to drag all that up again.

"Damn you Anna for a fool," she told herself aloud.

There was a knock at the door and the elderly butler entered.

"Telegram for you," he said holding it out on a tray.

"Thank you," she said.

He turned to leave.

"Could I ask?"

He paused at her question before nodding, "Yes Miss?"

"Have you seen Flynn?"

"I believe he's gone to the village Miss before going on to London."

"London? Why is he going there?"

"I wouldn't like to say Miss."

"To cause more trouble for me no doubt."

He shrugged non-commital.

"Could I ask, how do the staff feel about the changes?"

"Well, there's some worry obviously, but most are optimistic, and the rest you'll win round, but there are quite a number we're losing to the War, services, factories, etc, so the closure of the museum is a bit of a relief for the rest of us still here.

"Thank you."

She turned her attention to the telegram.

1.35PM YORK STATION TOMORROW STOP YOUR FRIEND O STOP.

Anna folded the letter and tapped it on the edge of the desk thoughtfully, letting the relief of having someone familiar around wash over her. News of London and Olivia's beau would be a welcome distraction. Although, she wasn't looking forward to possibly sharing the information that her brother had died with Johnson, in reality, she still hadn't decided whether she was going to share it with Olivia.

But, more importantly she must find a moment to ask Olivia about why she had left the hospital.

Anna turned her attention to the paperwork scattered all over the room, reminding herself to speak to Edward Blackwood about appointing a manager and Gerald the tenant farmer to get his advice.

Anna sat back and thought of the way her life had changed and how things were different now, from just a few weeks ago when her mother had died.

How she wished she could ask her for help right now.

Anna felt like she'd never needed her mother more and the waves of grief she'd been suppressing began to bubble to the surface.

She left the study and made her way to her mother's room, she didn't know why, but felt she needed to be there. And it was only there she gave in to the tears she'd held back for so long.

"Miss?"

Anna jumped to see a young curly haired girl bobbing at her in the doorway a worried expression creasing the girls perfect forehead.

"I have been sent to inform you that dinner will be served in 10 minutes, Miss."

"Thank you." Anna said attempting to straighten herself.

The girl nodded and paused, "Are you okay Miss?"

"What is your name?"

"Molly, Miss."

"Molly, did you know this room was my mother's.?"

The girls eyes went wide, "No, Miss."

"Who is in charge of cleaning."

"Why that'd the housekeeper Miss, Mrs Daniels."

"Where would I find Mrs Daniels?"

"I believe she's downstairs Miss."

"Excellent, could you take me to her, Molly."

The girl looked stunned, "Yes Miss."

"Molly, my name is Anna."

"Yes, Miss Anna."

The girl hurried off, Anna followed behind.

Molly looked anxiously behind her as Anna followed and she got the distinct impression the girl was scared of her, although she had no idea why.

Molly went into a room to the left of the narrow staircase and spoke to someone, Anna followed behind to see a stunned-looking middle aged woman with greying hair and spectacles perched on her nose.

"Miss," the woman said standing, "how may I assist you?"

"I wanted to just enquire as to why the room on the top floor is not cleaned?"

"I personally saw to the cleaning of your room, Miss, but if you would like I can send someone to do it again."

"No you misunderstand me, I mean my mother's room. Elizabeth Leyac's room."

"Oh I see," she paused. "That room isn't used as part of the museum and therefore cleaning is not done as often as the others."

"Would it be possible for it to be put down for a good freshen up? I was in there today and it's rather dusty and in need of some attention. Only if it's not too much trouble of course."

"Do not worry Miss, I can make sure that is taken care of for you."

"Thank you, and my name is Anna."

"You are welcome Miss Anna."

"I also have a visitor arriving to stay tomorrow, I'm not sure how long yet, but she's a dear friend and I'd like a room prepared for her if possible."

"Of course, I'll put her near yours, Miss."

Anna nodded and turned to leave.

"Oh Miss," Anna paused, "We're glad you're here Miss - welcome home. I hope everything is okay?"

Anna nodded and left with the distinct impression the woman could see she'd been crying and made a mental note to be more careful in future.

The following day, Anna found the journey to the station at York to fetch Olivia long and tedious. The roads were icy and frozen and the driver had to negotiate them cautiously and slowly.

The frozen icy fields and hills passed in a blur of white. The world like a glistening Crystal Palace of frost.

When they did eventually make it to the station, it was just in time to see the train from London pull into the station, it's long heavy carriages following the steam giant, as it slowed and came to a halt with a whoosh of relief.

It wasn't long before Anna saw Olivia's form gliding over the bridge; she spotted her and her ultra feminine manner from a distance and moved to greet her.

As they got closer, Olivia spotted her, "Anna Darling," she

held out her arms to Anna and embraced her tightly, Anna trying to breathe pulled back and smiled at her friend with genuine happiness.

"I'm so glad you're here Olivia, I can't tell you what a friendly face means. I feel like the enemy half the time."

"Well after you've dealt with large roguish uncooperative men as patients you can deal with anything."

Olivia hooked her arm through Anna's, "come on then darling, let me to the wolves."

Anna smiled and pointed to where the car and driver were.

"Ooh, hark at you with your own driver," she said as he took Olivia's case from her.

"Get in," Anna said shaking her head.

Olivia was fascinated by the view on the journey back, "so this is the north is it? Well I must say it looks much like the West Country. Not at all the run down place I expected."

"What did you expect?"

"I don't know exactly, I suppose I expected it to be much more rough around the edges and less, I don't know… normal."

"Olivia!" Anna said in mock shock, "Are you saying you expected the north to be backwards and unsophisticated?"

Olivia laughed, "I suppose I was."

"Well don't trouble yourself on that. It's exactly what I expected when I came here the first time. Now I can only say I am certain northern people only like us to think that, so we don't invade with our city ways."

"It is simply beautiful Anna, how do you not love it here, It's like a Bronte novel."

"It's cold, muddy and windy, Olivia, and miles from any shop with anything useful."

"Ooh grumpy Anna; just look at how the distant hills rise and fall then merge in the distance to meet the sky. And the icy frost, it makes it look magical. I feel like some rogue handsome chap will come and sweep me off my feet and I'll swoon in his arms."

"Olivia you really are too much."

"And you Anna are far to practical, you should stop and just breathe the beauty."

"Hmm," Anna said offering no further reply.

Some hours after Olivia had been safely settled in her room on the top floor next to Anna's, and had time to ooh and ahh at the house, how lovely it was, how she couldn't believe this was where Anna's mother grew up and where Anna was born, they settled into the drawing room with a pot of tea and, as she stirred the spoon in the teacup, she stopped Olivia's incessant chatter.

"Olivia tell me why you're here. I'm glad you are, but what's going on?"

Olivia paused mid flow with an, "Oh…"

Anna used the silence to pass Olivia her teacup and saucer.

Olivia slurped the hot liquid keeping an almost frozen smile on her face.

"I have the most wonderful idea for this place Anna darling, A convalescent home" she said.

"A what?" Anna paused her own teacup mid air ready to drink and stared at Olivia.

"A convalescent home, it's a kind of hospital, but for those soldiers and airmen who have severe injuries to mind or body and need special care and extra time to recover. This place is perfect, the setting is tranquil and it would solve your problem. Plus, it fills this great house with people so you're not rattling around here on your own."

"I don't want to be surrounded by people, and I'm certainly not up to looking after them, You're the nurse Olivia, not me. I would be terrible. Speaking of which, what happened at the hospital?"

Olivia continued ignoring her, "you don't have to nurse the patients, you would have doctors and nurses to do that. Some of those great rooms downstairs would make perfect wards for these people. you could separate the ones with shell shock from those with burns, and those with amputations. Anna it's being done all over the country and it will allow you to really help the war effort. Oh Anna, you need to trust me. Let me make enquiries while I'm here and we'll see what we can do, you don't have to make any decisions just yet."

Anna sighed "Olivia it really isn't for me."

This was the second time someone had suggested such an idea. She liked the thought of doing something useful with her new found privilege but not that.

CHAPTER SEVENTEEN

Anna

Following her conversation with Olivia, Anna again thought of Flynn. She had heard from Edward who communicated that arrangements were in hand and he'd be in touch again in a few days.

So, when Anna awoke from a fitful sleep the following morning, she decided she needed to try once again to communicate with Flynn and do something to help him come to terms with the situation and deal with some of the other things she'd been avoiding.

She sought out the elderly butler who had told her he'd gone to London and asked if he'd be able to get a telegram to him.

When he nodded affirmative, she asked him to convey a message asking Flynn if he was willing to come and have a meeting with her.

The butler bowed and left.

Anna knew she had some visits to make she'd been putting off; one to Sissy Jenkins' family and another to the Baxter's.

The Doctor's face flashed before her eyes and she pushed it to the back of her mind.

No, not him, she wasn't going to see him. All the same her heart flip flopped.

She was certain she could make both visits in one day if she was quick and she certainly didn't want to hang around in the Baxter's village any longer than she had to. Running into the doctor was not something she was keen on, although she should visit her mother's grave.

Maybe she should enquire about bringing her home to the estate. Although she had no idea of how to go about such a thing.

She pushed the thought to the back of her mind. The Jenkins family was going to be difficult to face, they had trusted her with their secret and the next thing they were aware of the article popped up in the paper. For all they knew, Anna could have done it herself and not told them the truth of the matter.

Yes that meeting was going to be very difficult indeed, but she needed to do it, if for nothing else other than decency.

When she reached the Jenkins farm and began walking down the muddy road she was happy to see the ground was now frozen and much easier than last time.

Margaret Jenkins' daughter was stood in the doorway her hands on her hips looking suspicious, until she recognised Anna, and her face changed to anger.

"Could I talk to you and your mother?"

"The last time I trusted you, you betrayed us, and the next thing we hear is an article in the papers. I knew never to trust a journalist. Go away before I do something I'll regret."

"I'm sorry how things worked out, but I had no idea about the article, my colleague betrayed me. Can I come in and explain? And for what it's worth I'm not a journalist anymore."

"Who is it?" a voice from inside called.

"No one mother."

"It's me Mrs Jenkins, Anna Forrester, I've come to explain."

"Let her in, I want to speak to her Dorothy."

"Mother you know what happened last time."

"I know and not many of them people come back afterwards, let her in."

Dorothy stood aside and glared at Anna.

Anna stepped over the piles of boots and wellingtons and into the bright warm kitchen.

Margaret Jenkins was sat in the same chair she had been last time, but she looked paler, more shrunken than when Anna had stood here, a mere few weeks ago, but now so much had changed.

"Come in, I have questions for you girl," Margaret instructed.

Anna did as she was told, and began speaking almost immediately.

"Mrs Jenkins, you have to understand I had no idea about the article,"

"Save your lies," Dorothy said behind her.

Anna ignored her and continued, "No it's the truth, I didn't I was betrayed by my colleague. Let me explain."

Margaret waved her hand to say Anna was to continue, and she told them everything, how she had found out the truth about her mother and how difficult it had been when she discovered what had actually happened to Sissy, who had in fact been loyal to the end.

Anna reached inside her handbag, "I've brought you the diary my mother left me. It gave me all the answers. She talks in detail of Sissy and their friendship. That's what I came to tell you, Sissy told you they were close and she was telling the truth. She died trying to protect my mother and me, and for that I only have gratitude for her."

Anna handed the diary to Margaret who took it with hands

shaking and tears rolling freely down her wrinkled face.

"I always knew she couldn't have done such a thing."

"I've marked the page where Sissy first comes into my mother's life. Sissy was her only friend during her pregnancy and was the one who ultimately helped her to escape, giving her life for mine."

Margaret Jenkins looked up from the diary then and stared at her.

"I'm also going to make arrangements for Sissy's body to be brought home to you so you can once and for all put her to rest. I hope this, in some way, makes amends for what happened and how the truth was kept hidden from you for so long."

Dorothy came and sat by her mother, who sat and cried with the tears of years of grief; years of not knowing pouring from her, as finally, after so long, she knew and could say goodbye to a beloved sister.

Dorothy spoke quietly, "Thank you for coming and telling us. It means a lot to know what happened." She gave the hint of a smile, which Anna took as a truce.

"I will leave you both now and, don't forget, if ever you need anything at all, get in touch, I will always be grateful to you because of what your sister did for me and my mother."

#

As Anna sat in the carriage on the way to Abbeyfleam, she smiled to herself; she was taking steps to put things right.

As the train approached the village of Abbeyfleam Anna looked around the area, thinking to herself that everything seemed familiar, yet strange.

The train slowed to a stop. Anna took a deep breath as the sun peered out from behind the clouds casting dancing shadows on the church graveyard in the distance. The cool breeze blew at her face and around her hair, gently lifting it from her neck. She glanced up the platform but couldn't see

Mr. Baxter, so instead headed straight to the church.

She moved to open the churchyard gate, which was firmly shut. It made a loud squeaking noise, breaking the silence and making her cringe.

Her heels crunched along the twisting path. The familiar smell of the place made her think of the last time she was here, when she buried her mother. The day itself an odd blur of mixed-up memories. As she reached the grave site and looked at her mother's fresh headstone she noticed the ground had been flattened and fresh turf laid across. Someone had put fresh flowers in the pot. She bent down and rearranged them. Satisfied she sat back taking a deep breath of damp fresh country air, the sun glistening off the top of the gravestone.

"Well mum I finally found out the truth. You know it would have been a lot easier if you'd just told me. I wish you were here now I've got the house. After all these years the Leyac house belongs to us. I didn't want it, as I'm sure you would have known, but things never really work out the way you want do they mum? Thomas is dead and I'm sorry for you and myself. I wish I could have met him."

Anna went silent then, just listening to the rustle of the trees in the wind. She could hear birds tweeting and from somewhere there was the hum of a tractor.

She listened to crunching footsteps and turned to see who was there, her heart leaping as Doctor Laker's figure approached.

She turned back to the grave site facing away from him, "Oh damn," she said under her breath.

Trying to steady her nerves she stood to greet him.

"Hello Miss Forrester," he said rather formally.

"Hello Doctor Laker, how nice to see you." She could think of nothing better to say and an uneasy silence fell between them.

"I often bring flowers to your mother's grave," he said rather obviously and shuffling his foot awkwardly.

"But really doctor, there's no need."

"I don't do it for you, like I said before, your mother meant a lot to me."

"I'm sorry I didn't mean to offend."

"No offence taken. What are you doing here anywhere?"

"I'm here to see Mr and Mrs Baxter. I haven't seen them since, well, since everything happened."

"Yes I see." He went quiet then and looked down at the floor.

"Actually doctor I'd like your advice on something…"

"Oh really?" His head shot up.

"I've fired Flynn but I'm still concerned about what he'll do."

"So you're keeping it then? Glad you changed your mind."

"Actually it was nothing to do with me. Flynn did it himself. He tried to make me disappear to Scotland."

"That's ridiculous…Come" he said. "Let me walk you to the Baxter's."

"There's no need I've got a car."

"Okay well then, goodbye Miss Forrester," he said annoyance crossing his face.

"Good day doctor."

He turned and left leaving Anna staring after him. She needed to get out of here as quickly as possible. She turned back to the grave once more,

"Goodbye mother," she said and left.

As she walked back up towards the Baxter's house, she could already see Mrs Baxter with a tea towel at the doorway, almost hopping from foot to foot in apparent excitement.

She wanted to laugh at how silly it seemed, but a wave of affection washed over her at the site of Mrs Baxter. She had been there for her when no one else had and almost adopted

Anna as her own. If she was truthful, Anna probably couldn't have done the house cleaning without her help.

Now she was back here, the grief was all too real once again. It had been easy to put it to the back of her mind when she wasn't in Abbeyfleam, but with each memory the sadness became overwhelming. This is where the whole investigation had started and where she first opened that diary. How things had changed since that day.

She waved back to Mrs Baxter with a smile and let the old woman embrace her tightly before steering her inside, and sitting her down with a big wedge of some kind of tart and a steaming mug of tea.

For the first time in ages, Anna felt she could relax for a moment, letting Mrs Baxter fuss around her, and sat back to enjoy a moment of not having any expectations of her, except to drink more tea and eat something.

Anna stayed much longer at the Baxter's than she intended and in the end had to leave before the trains stopped. The journey back was slow through the darkness, her stomach swirling with the copious amounts of liquid and food Mrs Baxter insisted she eat, as in her words Anna was, "looking mighty thin these days."

As she watching the darkened sky for signs of aircraft, she hoped Olivia had been all right on her own and found she was suddenly feeling very tired, the motion of the carriage and the silence making it difficult to stay awake.

Once back at the house Anna shivered in the cold night air and just a she mounted the steps, Dawkins called her. Turning, she shivered again as she waited for him to speak,

"You should know Miss, we've used our ration for petrol now and there's talk of a private petrol usage being stopped."

"So, no more car journeys then? Well it's no matter, it's not a luxury I've ever had before, so I won't miss it but thank you for collecting me from the station tonight."

Also, Miss, my call-up's come so I won't be here to drive you anyway."

"Thank you Dawkins and good luck."

"Thank you Miss," he said and got back in the car to put it away.

Anna went up to bed, yawning all the way up the stairs.

The morning light was grey and gloomy, a misty frost everywhere and Anna shivered as she sat alone, eating the food that had been prepared for her by the kitchen. She stared out of the window down into the gardens at the back and further still past the gates into the wooded area, now slightly obscured by mist, lost in thought.

She found she enjoyed the peace here and a calmness washed over her as if the house was finally settling into her presence and had decided it approved of her.

She ate quietly and drained the last bit of liquid from the teapot into her cup, setting the pot back on its stand.

She wondered then if she had made a mistake letting Flynn go so quickly before she truly had the lay of what was going on and how things worked here. But then the image of him admitting that it was him who had sent someone to kidnap, threaten and shoot her flashed into her memory and, again, she decided she had done the right thing.

She finished eating and moved from the room and up the stairs, intending to explore the library collection her mother had been so fond of, but the portrait gallery caught her eye and she stood and stared for a few moments looking at each portrait. Then she remembered, the portrait of Eliza stored away in the attic and smiled.

Quickly she descended the staircase, down to the staffing area in the basement,

"Do we have any strong men around? I have a portrait I'd

like fetching from the attics and putting up in the round gallery."

Anna took the two volunteers to where she had found the portrait. They moved the heavy furniture and dust billowed in clouds around them as they got to the portrait of Eliza and carried the large picture slowly down to the first floor round gallery. They leaned the portrait against a wall and one took out a dusting rag and began brushing some of the thick dust from the frame.

"Where is it going Miss?"

"I want it there, next to Lord Ashton, Lady Catherine and all the portraits following will need to be moved along to accommodate this one, back in her rightful place."

They stood back and surveyed the space, the older of the two, said, "We'll need to go and get the correct tools, and Joe, the repair man will arrange everything. Leave it to us, we'll let you know when it's done Miss," he smiled at her.

"Thank you for your help."

"Miss, she's very beautiful, I didn't realise the part of the story about her being the first Lady Leyac was true."

"Yes, it is, it's all true," she smiled "I'll leave this to you then."

She walked away, back towards the attics; there were boxes up there she wanted to explore further.

CHAPTER EIGHTEEN

Anna

Flynn stalked into the room removing his hat and throwing it casually across a nearby chair before moving to pour coffee from the pot at the side of the serving unit.

He took his cup, leaving the saucer behind and moving to the French doors that opened onto the garden.

Anna sat back picking up her own cup, setting her mouth in a thin line of determination, Olivia, next to her paused, her fork mid-air and mouth in a O, before composing herself and setting down the fork and folding her arms.

The silence lengthened as Anna waited for Flynn to speak.

Eventually he spoke to the garden view, "You wanted a meeting with me."

"Yes, I thought we might discuss the situation we find ourselves in"

He turned then moving towards her and seating himself at the table,

"You cannot win, you need me admit it."

Immediately Anna's anger rose, "Really Mr Flynn, and do you think you're irreplaceable?"

He shrugged then.

Olivia interjected,

"Anna darling, let's discuss this practically then we can all come to an arrangement that's agreeable."

Flynn looked at her as if he'd only just realised she was in the room.

"And you are?"

"My name is Olivia, I'm Anna's friend."

"Ah yes. The nurse."

Olivia raised her eyebrows. "And you're Julien Flynn I presume."

"Indeed."

"Now let's discuss this properly," Olivia said.

"Well it's simple really Miss Forrester, must stop being pig-headed and realise she needs my help and I simply won't allow her to ruin everything."

"Flynn you're just a power-hungry, money-grabbing leech and I won't have you tell me I can't do it because, let me tell you, I'll damn well show you I actually can."

"You silly fool, you have no idea what you're doing, you're just a stupid girl with no idea."

"And you're a detestable snake who wouldn't know manners if they bit him on the head. You're simply ridiculous."

"Ridiculous you say, well I'd say my concerns are justified."

"You think I like this situation, think I enjoy this. This isn't what I wanted."

"Well that's a lie, clearly you've had designs on this from the beginning. I was right to be suspicious of you from the start. You've taken what you wanted and don't care who or what you stand on to get it," he said standing up again and pacing the room.

"That's not true, at all. You were the one who ruined my life."

"Oh yes it looks pretty ruined from here, cozy in your big house and land, living my life, taking everything I've worked for just as I knew you would."

"Your life? What about mine? I've lost everything."

He laughed then, "Oh yes poor Anna, the extreme misfortunate of living in the Leyac house on Thomas' legacy, spitting on his memory."

"I just wanted to be a journalist and live the life I had before."

"You fool, people like you can't be journalists. When will you realise that it's over for you. You can never be a London reporter ever again. You're a Leyac, despite me wishing you weren't. You're not a journalist and you never will be, and you're not a patch on your brother."

Anna was muted into stunned silence then as she blinked back tears.

"And, I'm staying. I was Thomas' closest confidant and I won't let you ruin everything he built and stood for. You can live with it or leave."

He walked off leaving Anna and Olivia alone.

Olivia poured more tea in Anna's cup and pressed it into her hands as she sat wondering what on earth just happened.

They sat in silence for a long while until Olivia eventually spoke, "Anna darling, I think you may be angry with me."

"Why on earth for?" Anna asked confusion creasing her forehead.

"I've asked Doctor Laker to visit and help us with the current Flynn situation and none too soon it would seem."

"Oh, Olivia, why did you do that? He's the last person I want here right now. I've got enough going on without him complicating things."

"Well I think you don't know what's good for you and besides, it's too late now he's already said yes."

Anna felt the beginning of a headache pound at her temples and she moved to stare out the window and the dark grey clouds which again threatened yet more rain.

"Olivia you can't do this. I hope this isn't one of your ridiculous romantic schemes, it really isn't like that and the doctor agrees with me."

"Does he? Well don't worry, all will be well. He'll be an asset, you'll see, besides there's something I wish to discuss with him, as a fellow medical professional." She left the room humming to herself, leaving Anna alone with her thoughts.

Things seem to be getting worse, and she was further away from the life she wanted than ever.

Anna looked up again at the swirling clouds then below at the cold, wintery, spindly trees blowing and swaying in their barren state, and thought about the most recent letter she'd read from Eliza's collection:

My dearest Eliza,

I confess that perhaps my powers of persuasion have either lapsed or I simply need to see you in person and make you see sense. I mean, for goodness sake, your description of Leyac house and its surroundings seems dreary at best and not at all the magical place you say, but a wild dark place indeed. I feel myself baffled. What bewitchment is it that makes you feel what you say. I am determined to come and visit you and fetch you home again, this is simply nonsense. It is definitely not time, as you say, to grow up and stop acting like children.

Your loving George.

Anna looked towards the barren trees again wondering about George's relationship with Eliza and decided she must do some investigating once this mess with Flynn was sorted out.

As if the universe was conspiring against her, Flynn strode back into the room and paused in front of her.

"Do you know where I went when I left here?"

"London, I heard," she said turning back to the trees outside.

"Do you know what I did there?"he paused and Anna said nothing, "I made sure that you my dear, would never work as a reporter in London again."

Anna's head snapped up as she stared at him.

He laughed then, "I'm returning shortly, I have some unfinished business there, but I'll be back and you, my dear had better get used to it."

"Damn you, damn you to hell Flynn," she walked off leaving him there with a satisfied smile playing at his lips.

Anna paced the gallery, those words going round in her head.

How could he possibly have made sure she'd never be a journalist again?

He couldn't do such a thing.

He didn't have that kind of influence surely?

She continued pacing. Despite deciding to keep the house, she had always planned to go back to London.

But now had Flynn ruined that?

Well, the doctor hadn't helped on that score anyway; she thought back to him punching Marcus and felt a little satisfied that at least someone got punished for betraying her.

But could Flynn really take away the life she wanted?

What could she do now?

There must be a way to get back her career.

Then an idea formed, perhaps she could be a journalist closer to here, and not in London. Perhaps she could settle for the same job in a smaller more local environment, one where she could keep the house and still have a career.

She sped back down to the dining room in hope the local paper was still there. She was relieved to see it was and after scanning the pages she found the address and telephone number for their office in York. Smiling, she got her hat and coat and set off for the village.

Anna shivered in the cold air, the ground hard and frozen beneath her feet.

She stopped and turned at her name being called; Olivia was jogging to catch up.

"Anna where are you off to?"

"Just the village."

"Mind if I tag along? I have a letter to post to Mickey."

Of course," Anna said non-committal.

"Are you still angry with me over the doctor?"

"No, it's just something Flynn said but I'm determined not to let it get to me, in fact this trip is part of my solution. I refuse to allow that man to intimidate me."

"That's the spirit darling. I must admit, I find him rather a pussycat and not at all as ruthless as I imagined, but then he's no reason to have a quarrel with me."

"I suppose when you've dealt with tough soldiers and patients, it would take a lot to intimidate you."

Olivia laughed, "Indeed, that is true. I don't stand any nonsense on my wards."

"Olivia, tell me what happened." Anna asked softly.

"Don't ask me Anna, darling, I'd rather not get into all that dreariness."

"Okay, but I'd like to help."

"There's nothing to be done and it's simply too difficult to bring up, it's not something I want to think of. Just let me be here helping you and we'll save all that for another day."

They lapsed into silence before Olivia broke it with chatter about Mickey Johnson's last letter, to which she was now replying.

As they entered the village they separated, Anna to the station to use the phone in private, away from any possible eavesdropping, and Olivia to the Post Office.

Anna telephoned the editor and explained she was looking for a new position. It was only when he asked, "Why did you leave London?" that she paused.

"...I had to move here for family, but I'm a good reporter."

"What's your name Miss?"

"Anna..." she cringed, "Anna Forrester."

There was silence at the other end, so Anna filled it.

"I realise you might think me a difficult bet, but I just need a chance."

"I'm not sure. We're supposed to report the news not be in it."

"Could I come and meet you?"

"Hmm."

"Just for a chat?"

"Well okay, come down in a few days and I'll think on it."

Anna replaced the phone receiver in its cradle and smiled. Now she was getting somewhere.

She met Olivia and strolled back to the house. After a few minutes of silence, the two of them lost in their own thoughts, Olivia spoke. "Anna, will you reconsider giving Leyac house over to a hospital to help the war effort?"

"Olivia, I really can't see how that helps our current situation at all at the moment. I barely know what I'm doing and how to run a house, never mind whether to give it over for use. I really can't think straight Olivia. I'm just muddling through each day as best I can."

As they reached the house Anna noticed the doctor stood on the front steps waiting for them, his hat, coat and suitcase in hand.

Anna's heart lurched, but Olivia waved her arm madly, "Doctor, you're here."

He waved in return smiling at them as they got closer.

"I am so glad you are here, we're in need of help with Flynn, and a few other matters if I'm honest with you..."

Olivia continued, taking his case and striding into the house, the chatter fading into the distance as she disappeared inside.

The doctor and Anna just stood and looked at each other.

"Hello Anna," he said breaking the silence first. "It's good to see you."

Anna nodded, her throat dry, and she skipped inside after Olivia.

"Goodness doctor, what is in this case?" Olivia was saying now at the foot of the staircase.

The elderly butler, appearing then, took the case from Olivia, leaving her with a surprised look on her face.

He turned to Anna, "Tea Miss?"

"Yes, thank you," she said, "we'll be in the drawing room."

He nodded taking the case upstairs.

Olivia continued with the chatter and for once, Anna was glad of the distraction that interrupted the tension in the air between her and the doctor. As they passed the round gallery, he paused looking intently at the portrait of Eliza. Olivia turned and followed his gaze, moving to stand alongside him.

"Marvellous isn't she? Olivia breathed.

"So this is Eliza?"

"Anna's grandmother, yes." Olivia said smiling back at Anna who stood a little apart from them.

"She's mesmerising," he breathed. "It's the eyes…"

"Come," said Anna cutting off the conversation, "I'm sure tea will be along shortly." She moved through to the connected drawing room.

As they made themselves comfortable, the doctor said, "so what has Flynn been up to now?"

"I don't know, that's what's concerning." Anna said.

He nodded, "That is worrying."

"Then there's the other issue," Olivia chimed in.

"What issue?" he asked.

"Anna seems to be under the impression she can run an estate and be a journalist."

"Olivia."

"Well you do. And, I don't know how you're going to manage it."

"Easily, I'll go to work each day."

"But, what about this house?"

"What about it? Honestly Olivia, I don't want to deal with this now. I'm going for a walk."

She got up and left, heading for the gardens.

She hadn't been there long when the doctor followed her, his footsteps crunching across the frozen grass.

"I know you probably don't want to see me now, or perhaps ever, but I have always been honest with you and Olivia has a point."

"What point is that?" she said with a little more anger than she meant.

"You can't do everything and it's stupid to try."

"I'm not trying to do everything, I just want my life back."

"Well you can't have it, this is your life now and you should start dealing with it rather than this constant running away," he said his voice rising to match her own tone.

"I'm not running away from anything, why is it wrong to just want my life back?"

"Because you want something that's gone, and if you'd only open your eyes you'd see what a gift you have."

"There's no damn gift; it's a curse and I'm not letting it stop me be a journalist."

It's not about you, you fool. We're in the middle of a war, And from where I stand at the moment, the bloody Germans are winning, and while that's happening all you're concerned with is whether you can write stories. Don't you see Anna? Don't you see what you have?" He ran his hands through his hair in an exasperated gesture. "You could do so much more."

"They're not just stories, I helped people," she said quietly.

"And, here you can help so many more. Wake up Anna."

"What about what I want?"

"In wartime it matters little. Do you think the artist who dreamed of painting watercolours wanted to spend his days marching and shooting Nazis? No, he wanted to paint, but it's war, and war changes things. I want you to be my wife, but I won't ask you because I know it's pointless. I can't have what I want, I've accepted that, but I'll always be there to tell you when you're being a fool, and right now you're being a fool. It's time you accepted things the way they are. You're not a journalist, you're a Leyac. Now stop acting like a spoiled child and start acting like one for goodness sake."

"Sometimes I really hate you." She turned and ran to the house so he couldn't see how much his words had upset her.

She ran to her mother's room and cried until she fell asleep on the bed.

CHAPTER NINETEEN

Prisoner

He would have liked a bit more time to plan his escape properly, but knew it was only a matter of time before suspicions were raised, and he couldn't let that happen. His plans were set.

Laid on his bunk, he looked towards the window as evening drew in, noticing a few of the men huddled together in whispers, glancing at him sideways; he ignored it. He was almost certain the newcomer hadn't told Smith - not yet anyway. But, without giving him a good reason to stay quiet, why would he not say something?

The clock ticked by slowly, dragging like a millennial, one tick slowly following another, the evening dragging. How impatient he felt to get on with the task at hand.

It was risky but he was sure he could do it.

Slowly, as the evening turned to night, Johnson listened to the noises of men, moving about, shifting, wrestling and talking, slowly fading to the low hum of gentle breathing.

He waited, listening, straining his ears to hear, but only silence echoed.

Slipping out of bed quietly, making no noise, he tiptoed to

the back of the hut and disappeared through the side door.

It was frosty and his breath caught sharp in his chest, startling him more awake.

His mind wandered to Olivia and what she would think when she saw him. He pushed her firmly to one side; he couldn't let distractions cloud his judgement right now. He needed to focus on this escape.

He glanced around, saw no one and knowing the guard towers couldn't see him from where they were, he dashed across to the next hut and flattened himself against the back area. In the clear sky he could see the tiny shapes of bombers, and the distant thud told him there must be a drop site some miles away.

God he wished he could get up there in one of those planes right now, he closed his eyes briefly, as he remembered the magical feeling of being in the sky, free where there was no war, and the safety that in a very short time he'd be on home soil.

His eyes shot open as he heard a noise, but far too late. Smith and some of the others grabbed him by both arms,

"Hold him lads," Smith ordered in a firm but quiet whisper.

They dragged him back to the hut and he tried to wrench free but they held firm, and once back inside with makeshift blackouts at each window, Smith lit a dim lamp.

They forced him back onto a chair and held him there.

"Why were you trying to escape, Lieutenant, without committee approval?"

"I can't tell you. Let me go. I can still make it."

"You can't tell your own men, your fellow comrades in arms why you are escaping now, outside of the committee agreement, a committee you are a part of?"

Johnson remained silent as he caught the eye of the newcomer.

Had he done it?

Had he told them?

Damn him, he had no idea what he'd done.

"Our new friend here has told me some worrying news Johnson, some news I really don't want to believe, but I must say your behaviour tonight is not endearing you to allow me to prove he is wrong."

"Sir it's not what you think. You have to trust that I can't tell you. It's imperative."

"Imperative is it? what that you've been here spying on us for the enemy?"

"No. That's not true. I'm not a traitor."

Johnson felt a huge blow smack him square across the jaw, it stung all the more for being so unexpected and made his head ring. He sat back up and worked his jaw in a circle rubbing it with his fingers as he glared at Smith.

"You see Johnson, the evidence against you is quite difficult to dispute. You've lied, you've placed yourself on the escape committee, and all the attempts since you arrived have been foiled, and now we have a new airman arrive who tells me worrying information, and I have to say I don't like it."

"Sir, it's not what you think. There are good reasons for everything, but I can't tell you what they are."

"Really! You can't? Well we'll see how you feel after the lads have finished with you."

Smith walked off then, but before Johnson could speak again he felt another blow to his jaw and he pulled against the arms restraining him to try and return the punch, but couldn't wrench free, the restraining arms only gripping him tighter, with more force.

Another blow sent a wave of pain through his cheek and he tasted blood.

Damn it to hell, what could he do now?

* * *

Standing in the Kommandant's office in the morning light, he stared at the map of the world behind the desk.

The Kommandant pressed the fingertips of hands together and leaned forward, eyed him shrewdly.

"So Lieutenant, it has come to my attention that you're having some trouble with your fellow prisoners."

Johnson couldn't help but scoff and worked his jaw before rubbing his cheek, which he was sure was swollen twice the size. Talk about stating the obvious, he thought.

"What I want to know is why," he said drawing out the word why.

Johnson kept his face blank, but this was in part because it hurt to move it.

What was it they had told him to say if he was ever compromised?

It was then he realised the Kommandant had spoken again.

He looked blankly at him and the Kommandant sighed.

"You know it is only a matter of time before I discover what you are hiding. Or perhaps, you would be willing to tell me now?"

Johnson remained silent.

"Very well, I did not wish to do it, but unless you co-operate I will have to take further action."

The Kommandant signalled with his head slightly towards the corner of the room and Johnson saw out of the side of his vision a movement. Someone had been stood in the shadows - someone he hadn't noticed before.

Coming into full view now, his heart sank to his boots although he betrayed nothing on his face.

Schmidt looked at him carefully, a slight smile on his face.

The Kommandant spoke again. "Perhaps your fellow countrymen think you are a spy for us, but you and I both know that is not the case, so what is it?"

The Kommandant paused, "Tell me Lieutenant, have you

heard of Victor?"

Johnson froze inside at the sound of his code name, so he had been compromised by someone to the enemy, but shrugged lazily.

"Lieutenant, you might as well give it up, and tell us the truth, we know everything."

"Kommandant I know nothing of which you are talking. I have no idea what you could possibly be getting at. I simply had an argument over the football match and it got out of hand."

The Kommmandant leaned back in his chair, "Very well, have it your own way. Schmidt take him away."

Schmidt grinned greedily, and grabbed Johnson by the arm.

He wrenched himself free, glaring at Schmidt. He didn't have time for this. He needed to escape. Damn it all to hell!

CHAPTER TWENTY

Anna

The doctor's words had stung Anna deeply, more than she wanted to admit, so she spent a few days brooding on the subject and avoiding both him and Olivia. When it was came to the day she planned to meet the editor of the local paper in York, she slipped out early to avoid seeing his disapproving face.

But his words wouldn't stop swimming around her head, despite her attempts to quiet them, making her frustrated and angry.

Damn him. Who was he to tell her she couldn't be a journalist, him or Flynn for that matter, she thought while watching the country speed past, as she journeyed closer to the city, rain drops settling and running sideways on the train window. Her carriage was quiet and she was thankful for that at least, if only the doctor's words would stop hammering at her.

She would send him back to Abbeyfleam when she returned. He was just complicating matters and making things worse, and she would sit Olivia down and find out once and for all what happened to make her leave the hospital.

And with these decisions made she settled back wondering what this new editor was like and whether he would take her on. Yes, it was no Fleet Street but it was better than nothing, wasn't it?

But what if it's all boring work on recipes and cleaning tips?

Well she'd done that before, that was no problem. He might not let her write at all. He might just let her make tea.

No, surely not.

The train whistled as it pulled into the station and Anna pushed the thoughts aside as she got off and stepped onto the platform.

The cold wind wrapped it's way around her legs as she quickened her pace up the steps and over the bridge, descending the other side in a hurry to just get on with things. In her haste she ran into a soldier coming the other way. Anna noticed he had a crutch and despite it being Anna's fault, he apologised profusely while trying not to topple over and grabbed at the side rail, dropping his crutch to the ground. It clattered down the steps and landed at the bottom.

"I'm so sorry," she said bending moving to pick it up and only then noticing he had one leg.

"No harm done miss," he said smiling.

He looked about her age and Anna felt an immediate wave of guilt.

" Could I help you at all as a way to make up for nearly knocking you off your feet."

"Foot," he said smiling amused.

"Oh," she said smiling in return despite herself.

"I wouldn't mind a nice cuppa if you'd join me miss…"

"Forrester."

"Miss Forrester?"

"That sounds like the least I could offer you."

They made their way to the cafe on the platform and sat huddling their mugs, dished out by the WVS girls.

"You seemed to be in a hurry Miss I hope I haven't made you late?" he said.

"Not at all..." she realised with embarrassment she hadn't even asked his name.

"Webb, Miss, Joe Webb," he smiled.

"No you haven't at all. I can go later, it's not urgent, but might I ask where you were going?"

"I'm going home miss. As you can see the war's over for me now."

"You can call me Anna. Where have you been?"

"Been travelling up from the south coast. I was in a convalescent place there but I've been discharged now."

"How did it happen, do you mind my asking?"

"Dunkirk," he said simply shrugging and didn't elaborate. Anna didn't feel she wanted to pry further.

"Tell me about the convalescent home."

"Oh it was lovely, just lovely. Doctors and nurses there but it was in a house, a big one, so we, the other lads and me, didn't feel like we'd been stuck in some dingy hospital and forgotten about. We got to enjoy the outside, those of us able to, and it was just so much better than some dreary hospital with no atmosphere. There we could rest and get better in peace and comfort."

"That's very interesting Joe. So would you say these convalescent homes are vital to the war effort?"

"Yes indeed. All those kinds of places are. Some of the less injured ones made full recoveries so went back to their units, I can't do that obviously, but those of us who aren't going back, it was nice to know we were looked after properly. It helped us all immensely."

"So, if someone had the opportunity to give their house

over for such a place, you'd say they should do it?"

"Well, they'd have to have a big enough place and some are being requisitioned anyway, but yes, we all have to do our bit. From people like my old dad, who's a fire warden at night and still working during the day, through to lord of the manor giving his house for a school or base, and even those girls serving tea over there," he nodded behind at the WVS girls, "we all have to pull together, otherwise Hitler's already won and I've lost my leg for nothing and we can't let that happen."

"It's been lovely talking with you Joe but I must catch a train, I've got work to do."

"It's been nice chatting with you too Anna."

"Good luck Joe."

"You too."

She got up to leave and hurried back to the platform that would take her back to Leyac house.

She could hear the doctors words in her head and it was only now the fog had lifted, as if she could hear them properly for the first time. She had been so closed off to him - she'd rejected his words without a second thought.

She stepped onto the train and found a quieter compartment, looking out the window.

He had been right of course, typically, and Anna sighed at herself for her own stubbornness and desire to only listen to herself. It really was about time she admitted that she'd been wrong and she should have listened to practically everyone else, but particularly the doctor whose words had penetrated most of all.

She had been so focused on herself, she'd neglected to see what was right in front of her - that it was her job to make the best of the situation - to do what she could with the tools she had, rather than running around crying at what she wanted for herself.

She was so angry at her own stupidity, she spent the train ride back formulating a plan, so that by the time she stepped back through the door of Leyac house, she knew exactly what she needed to do.

Olivia, of course, was thrilled at Anna's decision and left to organise the arrangements of getting inspectors in while Anna telephoned Edward for an update and made arrangements to visit Gerald about his accounts. She was going to stop behaving like a child. She was taking charge.

After all she was a Leyac, like it or not, and it was about time she faced it.

Retreating to her room for a brief moment alone, Anna sat back on her bed and noticed the little bundle of letters, she looked at the scrawled handwriting on the next envelope, noticing the paper was brittle and browned in the light of her room.

She opened the next letter, listening as it crinkled and crackled.

My darling Eliza,

I am terribly saddened by the grave news you are to have a child. This is indeed a terrible blow. I find myself desperately heartbroken, for I know now there is no hope of you coming home.

Oh darling Eliza, I wish we could go to when things were simple, when it was just you and I fishing in the river, climbing and exploring, lazing in the sunshine. I feel like my right hand has been removed and no one told me how handicapped I would be. I'm not sure I can live my life like this.

What am I to do? Mother says, I must get up and find my vocation, but darling, what is that? Drinking copious amounts of whiskey seems to be a solution, but mother doesn't approve. Perhaps I shall visit Rome or even do the Grand Tour, what say you? Is it a good idea?

Your desperately depressed and miserable George.

Anna folded the letter. Was this the end of the relationship?

Did Eliza break it off when she found out she was pregnant?

George was unhappy about the child, perhaps Eliza wasn't happy herself, perhaps she wanted to go back to George?

Anna yawned and got into bed, she was exhausted and her brain fogged.

When she awoke, she thought of her brother and what his reaction to this might have been had he been alive. What would he have thought of her. She was still thinking of him when she moved along the corridor and stopped outside his bedroom door. So far, she'd avoided this room, as if it was some kind of intrusion, but was it an intrusion now he was no longer here?

She opened to door and peered into the silence.

His room was modest and neat compared with some rooms of the house. However, large expensive furniture told its own story of the room's privileged occupant.

She moved inside. On the surface it was quite impersonal, no photographs and a minimal amount of trinkets. He was clearly someone who liked order and simplicity. He didn't like fuss, she concluded.

His window overlooked the back of the house and gardens, and Anna stopped a moment looking out trying to get a sense of who he had been, a strange feeling of loss for someone she'd never met or known.

She shook her head and moved towards the bed and sat down looking around. The bedside table had a small drawer and she pulled it open.

Inside was a book, one Anna had never heard of before, a page about half way through was marked.

She put it back and moved to the wardrobe.

It was filled with shirts, trousers, suits and other mens

clothes.

She moved some of them aside absently looking at the things he wore, then she noticed at the back an old shoe box with an ill-fitting lid.

She crouched down and pulled out the box. It was filled with what seemed like school report cards. She read one from the stack.

Thomas Leyac could do much better if he concentrated on the lesson in hand and learned that we cannot only study the things he is interested in. Having said that, he can work very hard when engaged in a subject. He is a popular member of the group and the other boys respect him. He is confident and will happily take charge of situations when needed, but he can also work under someone and alongside other members of the team, a rare quality these days.

However, I did find his interest in the German Reich and Russian Communism a little unusual, but I am assuming that it is part of an interest in politics in general, and do not believe he is the kind of boy to join such movements. I wish him well as he leaves and I am sure he will do well in whatever he chooses.

Anna put the paper down, he had an interest in the Reich and communism?

What did that mean?

Anna shook her head, surely not, he couldn't have had Nazi sympathies.

She put the box back where she'd found it, frowning.

It must simply have been schoolyard curiosity, surely?

She now felt even less sure of who her brother had been than she had before. She was deep in thought as she went to the dining room but voices from those already there made her hesitate in the hall, that sounded like the doctor was already up.

Anna took a deep breath, she would have to face him sooner or later today.

She entered.

"Darling Anna, are you ready for today? The doctor and I were just discussing how to proceed and I have such a lot to get organised, I'd better start immediately."

Olivia left, air kissing Anna as she did.

Anna sat opposite the doctor and avoided eye contact as she poured tea into her teacup.

"I owe you an apology, doctor."

"You? You're apologising?"

"Is that so strange?" she said prickling.

"For you yes."

"Why do you insist on turning everything into an argument? Why can't we just be civil?"

"You are right, I'm sorry, apology accepted," he paused, "what changed your mind?"

"About requisitioning the house?"

"Yes."

"When I went to York to see the local editor, I bumped into a soldier who had lost a leg at Dunkirk. Over a cup of tea he told me how much his convalescent home had helped him after he returned home. Your words in the garden had been playing on my mind and it made me realise I'd been blind and self-absorbed. Everything you said was true."

"I'm glad to hear you've seen sense. And, does this mean you'd like me to stay a little longer?"

"Honestly, if you can aid us in any way I'd be glad to have you around."

He smiled then and drank the last of his tea.

CHAPTER TWENTY-ONE

prisoner

The prisoner awoke and could barely move; each inch of his body hurt and, feeling sick and weak, leaned over his bunk to try and make the nauseous feeling disappear.

Schmidt had taken him to the dark, dank underground room, with which he was becoming more than familiar, and had tried his utmost to get the prisoner to talk.

Luckily he hadn't stayed locked in the hole for long, but he also suspected that this was a ploy by the Kommandant to see what he would do next, but he was grateful, nonetheless, to be out.

He was determined they would never break him - more than one person's life would be in danger should he give in. But it could only be a matter of time before they realised what they had and he didn't like to think what might happen then.

As he sat shivering in that hole this time round, he realised he would have to break the rules and talk to Captain Smith, which would invariably put Smith in danger - the very thing he'd been trying to avoid, but sometimes situations just go wrong.

Perhaps, if he only gave Smith the barest minimum - but

even that was dangerous.

He felt tired, but forced himself to go to Smith, a long painful walk across the hut.

Sitting on the chair in the little cupboard that served as Smith's office, swaying slightly, his head spinning and his face feeling as if it was twice the size du to the throbbing sensation in his cheek that seemed to be growing, he took the tin mug of water Smith passed him and sipped as best he could, dribbling it down his chin.

Smith leaned back in his chair, "So Johnson, what can I do for you?"

"Captain Smith, what is your clearance level?"

Smith glared down at him, "None of your damn business, Johnson."

"Have you heard of Operation Chamomile?" His tone was hushed now.

Smith looked curiously at the prisoner before cautiously asking, "Why do you ask?"

"Well if you have heard of it you may also know of the operator that goes by the code name Victor."

"What of it?"

"Sir, Victor was an undercover operative sent over to retrieve vital information, however on his escape, the operation was compromised."

"Victor's information was lost, I heard."

"It's not lost, it's here with you."

The Captain's eyes narrowed, "And just how do you have Victor's information?"

"Because I am Victor."

"His eyebrows shot up, "…why didn't you say before?"

"Because it's highly classified, I shouldn't be here. It was a cock up, royally, the mission was compromised. But, I thought I could wait it out for an escape, except the new prisoner started saying things to make everyone suspicious, so now the Nazi's are onto me and they aren't stupid. They'll figure it out soon enough. I need to get out of here. That Schmidt is a bastard and no mistake. If he breaks me, that's it. Smith, you either have to kill me or help me escape, it's as simple as that."

Smith blew out his breath and drummed his fingers on the table.

"You could very well be a double agent? How am I to know otherwise? You say you're Victor, but I'm not sure."

"Look I've given you everything I can. I am who I say I am, and I may not be able to give you physical evidence - all I have is my word."

" I'm not sure whether to trust you or be furious."

"Put it this way, if you choose to not trust me and the government finds out you gave Victor to the Nazi's, it'll be your head on the block."

Smith thought for a few moments looking at him.

"All right then, I'll go with it, if you're not who you say, then our government will catch you anyway."

"Thank you Captain. First you need to calm the lads down and stop these rumours that I'm a Nazi spyTthat's what got the Kommandant on to me in the first place, and I need to disappear before they drag out every bit of info on our whole network from me."

"I'll get an escape plan organised immediately. We have some smuggled equipment we can use. Can you wait a few days?"

The prisoner nodded.

"I can get the cryptographer to send a message to London that we have information from Victor."

"Be bloody careful, Smith. Make sure it's encoded properly. The cryptographer - can he be trusted?"

"Absolutely, one of my own."

The prisoner nodded, stood and held out his hand to shake

Smith's, "You do understand I have put you in some danger telling you this, but I hope you see I had no choice in the end."

"I am prepared to take the consequences. I will make sure everything is done to get you out of here and back to London. But can I ask?"

Johnson nodded.

"What happened?"

"I was compromised before I'd even got on that plane. They knew just where to shoot us down that night. Someone on the inside passed info to the enemy. So far, they don't know they have Victor, but they suspect something, it's only a matter of time."

Smith nodded.

He turned and left then, to rest his aching body.

He was getting out, and soon he'd be home.

This time it was going to work.

CHAPTER TWENTY-TWO

Anna

On the day of the assessment, the group arrived promptly to look at the suitability of the house. A man with a rounded figure and heavy white moustache appeared to be in charge of the group. A young woman in smart heels with a notebook followed him scribbling frantically every time he spoke. Some other men followed also making notes and looking around.

The man and his group of followers continued to discuss and point at things which the young woman in smart heels wrote as they entered. The other men nodded and replied, which the girl also wrote down. To Anna's irritation, they completely ignored her.

After a few awkward moments, she moved towards the man and introduced herself.

He looked at her then blinking as if she had intruded in his house rather than the other way around, Anna suppressed rising anger and offered a smile of welcome instead.

He held out his hand and briefly shook hers.

"How do you do Miss, I have some paperwork for you."

The girl in the smart heels rifled some papers she was holding and produced one, handing it to Anna with a nod.

"This is your paperwork with all the particulars," he continued, "standard practice these days. I am going to assess the building and check it's suitability for the purpose you have requested, but I must say Miss, just because you have requested a hospital does not mean that is what you will get."

"Really? What else could I get."

"It depends on what is in demand, I shall let you know presently."

"I will require, the top floor to remain open to the family and I have some staff members already, and as this is me offering the house for the purpose of a hospital rather than a requisition, do I not have a greater say in how it is used?"

The man humphed and continued assessing the house ignoring her question.

Anna took an instant dislike to him. He looked down his nose at her.

The doctor touched her elbow sending an electric shock through her arm, "Let me handle this, Anna."

Anna nodded and she watched as the man greeted the doctor with far more respect and warmth than he had her.

She ignored the irritation in her stomach, this wasn't the first time she'd encountered this kind of behaviour, but something about this man really annoyed her.

She moved back to the dining room and poured another cup of tea standing at the doors to the garden holding her teacup in hand, staring down to the frosty gardens below.

Olivia paced as the men toured the house, taking in every aspect of the estate including the outside areas and gardens.

After a number of hours, Anna heard them return to the hall and the sound of muffled voices carried through from the hallway, by which time her teapot had already cooled twice and had to be refilled.

She heard them leave and the doctor came to find her.

"Good news, Anna, Olivia, they like the house and think the place, particularly the grounds will be good for convalescing soldiers. We have a yes."

Olivia squealed and hugged Anna.

"They want me to co-ordinate the refurbishment on our end and have said I can employ staff to assist me, so consider yourselves my assistants, they will be sending their own team along to inform what they require, and expect the first patients to arrive next week.

"Next week?"

"Yes Anna they are keen to get things moving immediately. We need to start moving furniture and storing the stuff we need to keep."

"I didn't realise it would be so quick."

"Yes we need to start today, we only have a few days before the first staff arrive. The doctor in charge will be first and he will see about staff. I will write and recommend you Olivia if you wish. Then, bed and equipment will arrive in two days time and the house needs to be ready."

"That would be fantastic doctor, thank you. Well, we'd best get started then," Olivia said.

"The whole ground floor will be given over to patient wards and a few small offices, so all furniture needs moving, the first floor drawing room will remain but will become a staff area, the first floor bedrooms will be changed into staff quarters and the top floor will remain the property of the family. The kitchens will remain the same, but some of the cellar rooms will be transformed into storage rooms for medicine and equipment, offices, a patient shower room, and other necessary things required."

Olivia jumped up and hugged the doctor, "Oh thank you so much, it's exactly what I was hoping for. Anna darling, I can stay here with you."

"We can store some of the furniture in the attics, some of it can be moved up to the top floor and we'll see what else we need to do. let's get organised then shall we."

Anna knew she'd have to make room for more people staying here, which meant boxing up and storing or getting rid of her brother's stuff.

Then there was her mother's room. She couldn't bear the thought of someone in it, so decided she would be the one to move out of her sparse guest room and into her mother's old room.

She decided that getting rid of her brother's clothes and possessions still felt like an intrusion when she didn't know him, but knew it had to be done.

She still felt an imposter and going through his things and disposing of them felt wrong somehow, so decided to store them in the attic to deal with permanently later.

There was such a lot to do, and there was no time for dalliances.

She thought back to when she cleared her mother's cottage and how helpful Mrs Baxter had been to her. It was an enormous relief to have someone with her during that time.

Leaving the coordination of the large furniture moving to the doctor, she went up to Thomas' room to get the hardest part out the way first.

She had got two staff members to bring a big trunk down from the attic to her brother's room and sat now on the bed looking at the wardrobe.

Olivia, came in.

"What are you doing in here Anna?"

"I'm clearing Thomas' things to make room. There's no sense in a room going to waste when we're going to have so many in need of one, and besides, he's dead, he's no need of this stuff anymore."

Olivia reached out her hand and squeezed Anna's. "So

why are you sitting staring at the wardrobe rather than clearing it?"

"Because I feel like I'm an intruder. I didn't know him and here I am packing up his most intimate possessions."

"Oh tosh Anna, I spend every day rifling through people's intimate garments in the hospital to deal with injuries and things. It's nothing more than stuff. It's not what really matters. Now come on I'll give you a hand."

She stood up and opened the wardrobe, beginning to take out items, and folding them neatly and putting them in the bottom of the trunk. The hangers clunked together as she returned them empty to the wardrobe.

Anna followed Olivia's lead.

"Didn't he have ever such a lot of fine clothes?"

Anna nodded rubbing the fine material of the jacket between finger and thumb. She really should be doing something with these, it's almost criminal to store them. But not yet, she pushed the thoughts aside.

"I feel positively scruffy."Olivia said holding up a dinner suit, it's bow tie slung casually half inside the pocket of the jacket.

As the wardrobe emptied and the trunk started to fill up, Anna began to feel a sense of achievement, almost as if she were exorcising one of the many ghosts in this house.

As one of the few moments Olivia and her were alone these days, she decided to broach the subject Olivia had been avoiding.

"Are you going to tell me what happened at the hospital and why you were put on enforced leave."

Olivia sighed and said nothing for the longest time, not meeting her gaze. She was just about to ask again when Olivia spoke,

"I don't want to talk about it, it was very bad."

"What? Worse than finding out your mother's some heiress

and you're a missing twin, who was supposed to have been a boy, and the owner of the estate tries to scare you off by having you mugged, kidnapped and shot at?"

Olivia laughed. "When you put it like that," she sighed, "I'd been struggling for a while, the long shifts, the difficult patients, then we lost one on the table - a young boy. I'd been speaking to him only a few hours earlier, it was supposed to be routine, such a sweet little thing he was, and then in a split moment, he was gone and that was it. I don't know Anna, I've lost many patients, and some of them tragic, but this one was really hard. I couldn't move on from it and my work was affected. In the end they suggested I wasn't cut out for theatre or emergency medicine and I'd be better off somewhere quieter."

"Oh Olivia, I'm so sorry, I didn't know this was happening to you. Why didn't you say?"

"You had enough to deal with and if I'm truly honest, I've been ashamed of myself. I'm trained for this, I should know better."

"I don't think you should be ashamed. Everyone has their limits. You've been dealing with the Blitz night after night for months. You've done shift after shift and been rushed off your feet for so long, it's no wonder you've reached a limit. It's only a wonder it took this long."

Thank you Anna. I appreciate it. Now if you're okay to finish off here, I'll go and see about what space we can make for some of the larger pieces of furniture."

"Yes you go. I've just got to go through the drawers and that should do it."

Olivia left the room and Anna sat alone thinking about what she'd just told her.

Olivia was stronger than most, but she knew a blow like that would really have knocked her confidence. Anna opened the drawers and pulled out notebooks, letters and other items. She didn't read them, just stored them in the trunk.

As she pulled out the last drawer it got stuck. There was something stopping it and she shoved and pulled it further to release it. She managed to open it a little way to get her hand into the drawer, feeling around for something jammed and scrapped her arm on the dark wooden edge.

She took her arm out frustrated and gave the drawer one last shove then pulled it hard in temper. It moved squealed and released throwing her backwards. The obstruction was a small folded envelope, which had been jammed down the side of the drawer stopping the drawer sliding properly.

It had been taped to the side but had come loose in all Anna's shoving and pulling.

Her heart pounding, she opened the letter. Neat handwriting filled the page, in German.

Anna's heart pounded. She didn't recognise the name who it was to or from, but had seen the handwriting before. She rifled through the trunk again and found it, an old exercise book from school, the name Thomas Leyac printed on the front she opened the book and compared, there was no doubt, he'd written this.

He'd written a letter in German to someone and signed it as someone else.

What was worse, it was dated only 9 months ago, that meant during the war.

Anna felt sick.

Was her brother a traitor?

And worse, was his death something to do with it?

CHAPTER TWENTY-THREE

Prisoner

He crouched in a clutch of bushes listening. The smell of damp mud and pine filled his airways as he tried to catch his breath. Had he been followed? Was that footsteps.

No.

No there was nothing but silence, and the sound of an owl hooting made him look up at the cloudy night sky. The moon was hidden behind a patch of deep cloud and provided some welcome cover in the dark evening. His breath caught as he pulled in sharp, cold night air and tried to steady himself.

Peering out of his hiding place and glancing back towards the camp, daring to believe his eyes that yes, he was out and touched the cold hard ground beneath his fingertips.

He hadn't been spotted, so keeping low and steady, he moved away into the trees, his training instructor's voice popping into his head as he remembered the way he'd yelled if any one of them had got it wrong, "A mistake like that and you'll be dead," the instructor had shouted at one man.

Forcing his attention back to the present he quietly darted further into the woods and away from the camp.

Hopefully Smith would have been able to let London

know and MI9 would provide some help to get him out of here.

Damn, he did miss home. He pushed the thought to the back of his mind. Not long now.

He had to focus on what he was doing if he had any hope of not getting caught.

Moving steadily for a few hours his first aim was to put as much distance between the camp and himself as possible, so he followed the woods parallel with a road, cutting though the middle and snaking through the woods, all the while heading west.

He continued on until the early dawn keeping the road to his right. As dawn began to break, and the early morning birds tweeted, he felt more exposed, despite the cover of trees. He needed to think what to do next but knew he couldn't afford to stop. Patrols would be out looking for him soon, if they weren't already. He couldn't afford to wait until darkness - the place would be swarming. He paused to re-examine his directions.

Voices travelled through the trees and he froze, crouching down behind a large trunk, listening.

The voices were faint but female, he was sure of it. He moved slowly towards the sound keeping himself hidden and silent. It was a painfully slow process, but as he moved his head above the bushes and peered ou,t he was almost amused at the sight.

A group of nuns were by the side of the road arguing over a steaming car engine. One was arguing it was the other's fault for not checking the car before they left, another said it wasn't her fault as she hadn't been told to do such a thing, another was studying a map and looking confused.

Johnson watched them for a minute, wondering whether he should reveal himself, after all they were German, and most likely were loyal to Hitler, but then, he could always steal the car. If he pretended to give himself up, fixed their car he could steal it and get away. The thought of the soldiers out looking for him made the decision, the promise of a vehicle to get away faster was too much temptation to ignore.

He paused for a minute, wriggling his toes in his boots, the ground was frozen and he was starving and desperately needed to get out of these woods. He stood up, his hands in the air, and spoke to the nuns.

"Tut mir leid, ich bin Offizier englischen RAF würden Sie mir helfen? Ich kann das Auto für Sie zu reparieren, wenn Sie das tun?"(I'm sorry, I'm an English RAF officer would you help me? I can fix your car for you?).

The nuns stood frozen for a moment staring at him open mouthed.

He began to move forward.

Suddenly the one with the map blinked and set her face, "Halt!"

He did as commanded.

"Englischen?" The one peering over the engine asked him.

"Ya, RAF," he replied.

"Dein Deutsch ist gut," the one with the map said suspiciously.

He told them he had learned German at school and had been good at languages.

"Where is your plane?" she asked scanning the sky above.

He told them he had escaped from a camp and was heading for England and repeated again that he could fix the car if they helped him.

He was beginning to get nervous now, stood out in the open road like this, all it would take would be a patrol to come along and that would be it, the game would be up.

"Bitte," he pleaded with the women trying hard not to panic and just run for it.

The third one had large thick glasses and peered through

them. Up until this point she'd remained silent but said she thought they should let him fix it, she was hungry and didn't fancy standing outside freezing to death, when there was someone here to help.

The one with the map repeated that he was 'Englander' and looked at him a little resentfully.

The one with the glasses said she didn't care where he came from and the Lord had sent him to test them.

The one with the map said he was the enemy.

The glasses one, said that no, he was Hitler's enemy not God's and God had sent him to them, this was a test and they should obey.

The other one looked from one to another and then held out a spanner towards Johnson, he didn't wait for them to change their mind but plunged right into the engine trying hard not to let the relief show too much on his face

CHAPTER TWENTY-FOUR

Anna

The next few days were a blur as the house changed from a museum into a hospital. Medical equipment arrived and the ground floor took on a clinical smell as each new piece arrived and the rooms prepared, as if the house itself were changing identity.

As a series of staff arrived, settled in and the house became full of people, Anna took to wandering outside in the gardens more and more to escape the chaos. Her thoughts strayed to her mother and she again wished she was still alive to help her deal with this whole situation. She still felt a huge sense of displacement, as if someone had taken her life and put her in someone else's. She wondered what it would have been like if her and her mother, and her now dead twin, could have grown up together.

She dismissed these thoughts as the doctor called her in to make a decision on some other item of furniture that needed careful handling. She had no idea what she was doing, she knew nothing about priceless furniture.

"Oh and Anna, could you let me know what you want me to do with all the signage?" he called as she attempted to retreat away.

"What signage?"

"From the museum, the information and signs that we have removed from the walls all over the house to give visitors information."

"You can get rid of them, I have no need for them, the house won't be a museum ever again. And doctor, can I ask?"

He nodded.

"You've been amazing help but don't you have to get back?"

"Soon I do yes," he said and left.

Anna spent the rest of the morning trying to find space for all the furniture that had been removed from the ground floor, and didn't notice at first the figure standing in the corner.

It was hearing her name called in that familiar voice that made the room still, the scene playing like a movie from which she had become removed. She turned to peer into the smiling face of Marcus.

"Hello dear. How is life as lady of the manor. I see you're already making yourself at home."

"What the hell are you doing here?" she said walking out the front door.

Marcus followed.

"I was hoping for a little favour, for old time's sake."

"You must be joking. Get off my property Marcus. You're not welcome here."

"You can't hold a grudge surely. You only have it because of me," his tone changed then, "if it wasn't for me you'd still be a failing hack."

"I was a damn good journalist. You ruined that. I'm picking up my life as best I can, no thanks to you."

"Oh I'm sure you are picking up your life, famous surname, a fortune in the bank, a big house and staff to boot.

Yes poor Anna Forrester, so hard done by."

Anna marched across the circular driveway towards the gates, with him following,

"Get out Marcus, before I have you thrown out."

"Not until you give me an interview. Come on, tell me what you're doing here."

"No chance Marcus," she stood by the gates and turned to face him, pointing towards the exit, "Leave now, before I have you thrown out."

"Alright, I'm going, but I'll be back. I always get my way and I always get my interviews."

"Not with me you won't," she said and turned marching back to the house, her fists clenched.

"Did you know Flynn's in London?"

Anna stopped but didn't turn.

"I've seen him."

She turned and looked at Marcus' face. He leaned back against the gate and lit another cigarette, blowing smoke into the air before answering, "and I'd stake my life he's up to no good."

"What makes you say that."

"He was in a rough part of town."

"Well you must have been there yourself to notice him."

"Well, I'm a reporter, there's good reasons for me to be in a place like that, but him…"

He took a drag on his cigarette and shrugged leaving the rest of the sentence hanging in the air.

"And some of the fellas he was mixing with, well… let's say I'd watch out if he's still after you."

"I'm not scared of Flynn," she said instinctively, but there was no doubt the news sent a shiver of cold down her back.

Marcus shrugged and left, "I'll see you around Forrester."

How dare he?

Who does he think he is?

As if I'd ever give an interview to the person who was the means of ruining my career.

But then there was Flynn. She knew he'd not given up and it seemed he had been busy again in London. Last time he told her he'd made sure she'd never work again, but now what was he up to? She shook her head, pushing Flynn from her mind as she returned to the house, but nevertheless, still a little unnerved by the news.

To stay out the way of the commotion she retreated to the attic to organise things better and after pausing in her room to change clothes and wrap her hair in a scarf, she set off up the stairs.

Pushing her way to the back she began stacking the older boxes and a strange ancient rocking chair in a way that meant the newer pieces could be moved into the space she made giving the place more room all over.

She had no idea how many hours she was up there and was just about to leave when she knocked into a large stack of boxes banging her elbow . The box on the top of the stack fell and split open, its content spilling on the floor. She cursed and picked it up, as she did more contents fell out - a mix of knickknacks and clothes which she piled haphazardly. But they were strange looking somehow, Anna couldn't quite put her finger on it and began holding each one up as she put them in the box, a frown crossing her face.

It was only when she picked up a jacket and a little folded note fell out that she began to realise what was wrong, these clothes, the cut they were distinctly European. Nothing wrong with that, her brother might have liked the cut, doesn't mean anything, she thought, picking up the note.

My dear Lord Leyac,

I assume you got back okay from last night's rally. It was a riot wasn't it? But do not fear those who interrupted and tried to break us, they will not succeed. The black shirts will stay strong and with you we'll all prevail. I am honoured you've taken an interest and hope we can chat further soon.

Your friend M.

M?

Mosely?

Her brother was a black shirt?

And with what she'd found in his room about his obsession with fascism at school, Anna was almost certain her brother had been a traitor.

For the first time since she'd found out who she was, she was glad her mother was gone and not able to see what her son had become.

CHAPTER TWENTY-FIVE

Prisoner

He didn't want to admit it but he had always been someone who rode horses more than drove cars, but how hard could it be?

He swallowed, keeping his face neutral and peered through the steam at the engine.

He needed to get this fixed quickly, before a patrol came along and looked nervously along the road.

The nun who handed him the spanner, must have seen the glance because she asked if they would be looking for him? He looked up into her piercing blue eyes and nodded.

She sighed and bent over the car engine alongside him. After what seemed like forever, Johnson and the nun, both now sweating with perspiration despite the cold, finally got the engine back into a nice roar and he couldn't remember ever hearing such a wonderful sound, he grinned at the nun who smiled in return.

They secured him in the footwell of the back seats and two of the nuns sat with their habits spread out, covering him completely. He crouched beneath their skirts while the other drove, his legs and back protesting. He felt the car move and judder over the bumpy road and, despite his predicament, thought it amusing that he was in a rather compromising position beneath the skirts of two nuns.

They drove for a little while and he shook away pins and needles in his fingers.

He ignored the cramping in his leg and the aching of his arm and listened intently as the car slowed suddenly and the nun in the front spoke with someone.

Johnson held his breath as a voice asked if they'd seen any escaped POW's on the road, the nun replied they hadn't and Johnson heard a curt "Danke, Heil Hitler."

"Gott segne Sie."(god bless you), the nun replied and he felt the car move on again.

He let out his breath in enormous relief.

Well if they were going to give me up that would have been the time.

It was some hours later when Johnson was awoken, he must have fallen asleep, lulled by the engine.

As he blinked confused, it took him a moment to realise whose faces were staring down at him, his leg was numb and his arm painfully sore from laying on it. He straightened up, his body feeling like a crooked old man, and slowly, as sleep gave way to rational thought he remembered what happened.

He was in the courtyard of a large grand monastery, made from stone but worn, its grandeur now tired and drab. It looked damp and cold but he was more than happy to see it.

"You are safe now," a new nun spoke in heavily accented English, who had appeared from an adjoining door.

"Danke," he said.

The woman looked surprised at his German but said nothing.

They took him on a confusing round of corridors, stairs

and rooms to a remote room with a bed.

"You can rest here, food and a bath will be drawn for you, but for now, rest. It will be a few days before we can organise your transport."

"Thank you. I know the risk you take helping me." he said to her retreating back.

She turned and looked at him shrewdly.

"God does not distinguish between his children, only us flawed humans do such things."

"Thank you all the same."

She smiled and left, closing the door softly behind her.

He was left in silence, a silence that unnerved him, even in the camp at night there hadn't been true silence. It was the kind of silence that is heavy in its emptiness, and it reminded him of home - those nights when the world seemed to pause and everything stood still.

He kept his mind on his escape and pushed those thoughts away, busying himself checking the room and cautiously peering out the windows looking all the time for anything that might be a betrayal, anything that could be a trap.

Satisfying himself he was okay he warmed himself by the fire, truly relishing in real warmth, thawing out those frozen memories of what it truly felt like to be deliciously warm.

The crackling and popping made his shoulders relax slightly and he suddenly felt tired, bone tired, and could almost relax enough to fall asleep sat up.

A knock brought him back to the present and a young shuffling sort of girl in a postulant's habit came in and told him they had brought his bath.

He nodded and she opened the door wider. The one with the blue eyes who had rescued him came in carrying a tin bath, the other two came in with jugs of water, which were poured into the tin contraption and towels and fresh men's clothes were laid on the bed.

"Food will be brought in 30 minutes once you have finished your washing," the blue eyed one said before she left the room.

Alone again he looked amused at the old fashioned tin bath and smiled, it may be crude but it was better than what he'd been getting at the camp. He stripped and sat in the water laying back a little as best he could with his long limbs.

They had left him, soap and shaving implements and he reached for the little mirror and peered at himself. He had aged in the last few months and was shocked at his refection. Ignoring it he began lathering up to shave.

He did find it more than a little concerning that the nuns had men's shaving equipment and clothing so easily to hand, and made a point to find out why that was.

It made him wary. Was this a trap?

He continued washing, feeling like he was washing off the camp enjoying the chance to feel properly clean for the first time in ages.

By the time he had finished pulling on the trousers, which were a little large, but serviceable, the nun he met when he arrived had returned with a tray of food for him and began clearing away his washing things.

"Once you have eaten you should rest, we will talk in the morning," she said and left.

Over his food, his thoughts strayed to Olivia. He would tell her himself, he decided. It was the only decent thing to do. She would probably be very angry but he hoped she would understand.

Yes he would sort everything out once he got back on English soil, he thought, spooning a mouthful of food.

It was bland and basic but filling and much more substantial than the camp rations. He laid on the bed intending to shut his eyes for a moment.

* * *

He awoke much later, disorientated at his surroundings and jumped from the bed alert, eyes wide with the startlement of one woken from a deep sleep. Slowly as his brain caught up with his body, he heard the noise which had woken him, a faint knock at the door.

"Come in," he called in German and the door opened.

The nun with the blue eyes who had rescued him came in with a tray of breakfast.

"You slept a long time," she commented, "I returned last night and you were sleeping."

His stomach growled at the smell of the hot food, but he cautiously looked at her as she entered and set the tray down on the table.

Had he really slept from early evening, through the night?

"What time is it?"

"Almost five," she said.

As she turned to leave, he called to her to wait.

She turned and looked at him expectantly.

He decided that the best way would be to come right out and say it.

"I find it interesting that you happen to have men's clothing and shaving utensils in your monastery of female nuns."

The question in his voice was clear.

"You are not the first."

His eyebrows shot up.

"Do not look so surprised, we have also been checking up on you too. We have to be careful that you are not a Nazi spy trying to compromise our safety. Lucky for you, your story is true, but if it had not been," she paused "let me just say that you have had a weapon trained on you all the time you have been here and if necessary we would have used it."

He raised his eyebrows at this and found it more than a little amusing these women weren't as innocent and non-political as he had assumed they were - the perfect cover.

"Eat quickly, there is someone here to speak to you."

"Who?" he asked, moving towards the food laid out on the tray and beginning to eat.

She shrugged and left the room. He turned his attention to his meal and had barely finished when a man in very shabby trousers and old jacket came in to the room. His hair was longer than usual and he wore it swept it back from his face. His eyes were sharp and darting, as if he had assessed Johnson in seconds.

When he spoke it was with a heavy French accent, "I am Pierre."

Johnson cautiously moved to shake his hand, but instead of taking his hand Pierre, drew back his fist and in an instant slammed it hard into Johnson's stomach. The move caught him off guard and made his eyes water, his freshly eaten meal threatening to come back up. His first instinct was to let out a stream of swear words at the intruder.

However, Pierre looked amused and before Johnson had time to recover and retaliate, he said, "I apologise my friend, it is a necessity to test your story."

"A likely story..." Johnson moved towards him with the intention of giving Pierre an equally hard blow.

"I am resistance."

He stopped and looked at him with incredulity, "Why the hell did you hit me, you bloody crazy Frenchman?"

"I test all like this, it is a way to see what your reaction will be, I find it a good way to see. My dear Englishman, if you had been a Nazi spy, you would have immediately lapsed into German swear words when I hit you but you did not, therefore I can asses that you are indeed English and I will help you. You must understand, we have to be very careful."

Johnson shook his head rubbing his sore stomach. Crazy Frenchman, he thought, still in two minds whether to hit him back. It was only that he didn't want to waste good food that made him swallow down the breakfast still threatening to come back up.

"Now we go," Pierre waved at Johnson to follow.

"What now?"

"Yes now."

"Where are we going."

"It is best you know as little as possible."

Johnson realised he had little option but to trust this strange Frenchman, but all his senses were telling him to be cautious and he wondered whether he would have been better staying alone in the woods, making his own way back.

But, he had to trust Pierre would do as he said and not just hand him in to the nearest patrol.

The Frenchman took him by dilapidated farm vehicle down a series of winding roads and through hills so it seemed all they were doing was driving round in circles, but he noticed Pierre had avoided any checkpoints and patrols.

Suddenly, Pierre took the vehicle off-road down an almost hidden dirt track. The truck bumped and juddered and Johnson was sure it would get stuck, but as the track twisted downwards it came to a run-down farmhouse with half its roof missing. It clearly wasn't used much as a farm these days but would once have been a rather comfortable estate. Pierre pulled the vehicle to a halt with a harsh slam of the breaks and jumped out.

Johnson followed, wondering if inside would be a patrol of guards, but decided that Pierre could have found a much easier way to hand him in if he'd wanted to.

Pierre opened the front door and held it back gesturing with his arm for Johnson to enter.

He did so, cautiously, listening and watching.

There was nothing.

Silence thick on the air.

He moved forward, his footsteps the only noise in the gloom. Behind him Pierre shut and locked the door, Johnson's heart raced, this must be a trap. Any moment now a whole patrol of Nazi's would jump out.

"The door on your left," Pierre told him.

He looked back trying to gauge Pierre's expression and found a bored blank look, only his quick sharp eyes giving him away.

Johnson took a deep breath and braced himself taking hold of the handle and pushing the door open, standing his ground ready to run.

Inside were a host of people, smoking and laying around looking more than a little bored.

The surprise on his face must have been evident, because Pierre, laughed and pushed him into the room.

"Sit, sit my friend,"

A hard kitchen chair was offered and Johnson sat, all eyes now on him.

Pierre sat opposite and lit a cigarette, blowing smoke through narrowed eyes as he watched Johnson - eyes meeting his shrewdly.

The next hour passed in a blur of questions and more questions, Pierre and the others examined and cross examined him.

A problem arose when they tested him by asking the number of the bus that ran from Baker Street to the Zoo. Of course, Johnson had no idea and they assumed he was a spy.

Pierre, however wasn't convinced he was a Nazi, despite the fact he spoke excellent German.

The woman in the room, had taken a dislike to him and said they should shoot him to be safe.

In the end he had to tell them to check with MI9 whom would corroborate the details he gave them, he told them to say they had Victor.

They went away and some while later came back and offered him a cigarette.

"So, it seems MI9 are keen to get you back Victor," Pierre said.

"That's not my name, it a code name"

"I am aware of this," Pierre said.

"We never moved a spy before, most are too good to get caught," the insinuation clear.

Johnson just shrugged and instead asked, "When can we move."

"Tonight," Pierre said.

CHAPTER TWENTY-SIX

Anna

A few days after her unfortunate encounter with Marcus, and his worrying words about what Flynn was up to, and her discovery in the attic of what she was now almost certain was evidence of her brother's treason, she found a welcome distraction with the new patients.

Anna was finding spending time with the soldiers really rewarding, and her journalists instinct meant she had become quite adapt at getting some of them to share their story with her, she was rapidly becoming the one they complained and expressed their worries to, or for those who never got letters, the one they looked forward to chatting with.

There were some however, whose physical injuries were only the tip of their suffering and some of those sat quietly, not moving or speaking. Often, they were transferred to specialist places.

The doctor in charge, doctor Wilson, was an efficient man with a good instinct, but lacked any empathy that Anna could see. However, Olivia fitted in well in her new role as ward sister after a successful recommendation from Doctor Laker. All the patients looked up to her with respect. Anna had been watching her with interest as this new efficient, no-nonsense Olivia took charge of all the nursing needs. Even Anna dared not defy Sister Olivia in her starched uniform and hat.

There was one soldier, the newest on the ward, Anna was most curious about. His hands shook but he was equally just as happy to talk to someone. Anna presumed it was to take his mind off things. He had grown up in the country and talked about how he used to get up early and feed the chickens. His childhood stories were filled with long summer days and exploration, little boys fishing in streams for tadpoles and climbing trees. Anna found his voice lulled her into a sense where she felt she really could see the images he was painting in her mind. She had began to look forward to their chats.

As Anna approached his bed, she saw he was frowning, hunched over papers in front of him, muttering.

"What's the matter Stan?"she asked as she pulled the chair closer to his bed, in what was once the dining room and where portraits and chandeliers still told of the grand house beneath the surface of the hospital facade.

"It's this letter," he said throwing his pen down onto the bed sheets.

"Are you writing to your girl back at home?"

"No I can't do it."

"Well let me help, I used to write for a living," Anna smiled.

"It's not the words that are the problem, it's these," he held up his hands in the air.

"They won't stop and I can't write a word. I'm a useless, good for nothing who's gone soft in the head," he said the frustration evident in his voice.

Anna watched as he held his hands tight to try and keep them still, "Well let me write it for you, you just tell me what to say, and you're not useless, or soft in the head."

He grunted but didn't say no, so she persisted reaching for the pen.

He sighed, "I wouldn't want to impose."

"Nonsense, I'm more than happy to help. It's not like I've got a career anymore, you'd be doing me a favour. I miss holding a pen and writing. I don't even have any family to write letters to anymore. So I'd really like to help."

He smiled with evident relief and handed her the notepaper and pen.

She sat, pen and paper poised in front of her and looked up at him expectantly.

"Dear Violet," he said.

Anna wrote the words and looked up at him, he was watching her, she smiled encouragingly and he continued.

"I got your letter and am pleased the village voted with you on the recent elections. I'm happy you've now got the leader you wanted for the WI. Make sure you save some of that jam for me, don't sell all of it. I haven't tasted jam in so long, I found I could almost taste it when you were telling me in your letter last month."

He paused while Anna caught up with his words. She looked up at him when she had finished.

He smiled.

"My leg is getting better and shortly, I should be able to see whether I can walk on it. We won't know the long term effect until I've tried to stand, so I will keep you posted on my progress but the doc is hopeful. However, my hands keep shaking so I am having to dictate this letter to a very nice lady who owns the house where the hospital is. Lady Leyac, although she prefers Anna, has been really good to me and has made my stay here more bearable.

We are getting some nice dinners, but anything is a sight more tasty than a ration pack. So you see, you have no need to worry. I am next to a jolly chap who I am becoming very friendly with, so we're quite a merry bunch on the whole. Do keep me posted on news from home. Your loving husband, Stan."

He paused while Anna finished writing, "Does that sound alright?" he said when she looked up at him.

"Yes it's a lovely letter. She'll be very pleased with that and I think you will have alleviated some of her worry for you."

"Thank you Miss."

Anna nodded and stood handing him the finished letter and he looked down at it smiling.

As she left the room her mind was already on Eliza's letters and whether they were actually from a lover. If she were honest it was also in part to avoid thinking of her brother's treason. She had decided she would start her search at the library in York, go through the archives and look at some books on the military occupation of India.

She also thought it might be a good idea to look at the personnel archives but she was unsure whether she would be able to get access to these. Perhaps the ferrety man might have some documents relating to Eliza's family and friends hidden away somewhere. She paused to call his office from the green room, now the new doctor's room, and found him just as irritating on the phone as she did in person.

When she explained what she wanted there was silence on the line, she was about to repeat the question when he did finally answer, his voice now hesitating and cautious, which made Anna all more suspicious.

I'm determined to find out the truth she thought as she pushed him until he agreed to meet her in York and tell her what she wanted to know.

Her disastrous misplaced trust in Marcus had made her wary, she wasn't about to make the same stupid mistake twice.

She replaced the receiver and paused for a minute listening to the sounds of the place, alive with activity and certainly not the bleak prison her mother had described - not anymore anyway.

She was still considering her mother as she walked into the Central library and began perusing the shelves of books on India. She flicked through one absently but it had no useful information except on geographical positioning. She replaced it, opened another. This one talked of how to run a proper household with a checklist against the inside. Another told how ladies should be careful of the hot sun. It told of the food and the people, she slammed it shut, she was looking in completely the wrong places.

A ding of a clock striking the hour made her look up, It was almost time for her meeting with the ferrety man and Anna was dreading it.

As she approached the cafe where they were to meet she could already see the ferrety man through the window waiting and fidgeting over his drink. His hands were twisting around the cup and spinning it in its saucer.

He looked up when she approached his table and almost knocked his drink over trying to stand and do a strange nodding motion with his body as she sat opposite removing her gloves.

"Ah Miss Leyac, please sit. I have the information you asked for."

He patted his briefcase and Anna nodded and turned her attention to the waitress who had appeared at her side. She ordered a tea.

The waitress left and Anna turned back to the ferrety man who was now rifling in his briefcase.

'I'm afraid there's not a lot of information on her, she was the daughter of a military man stationed in India, a Major I think by all accounts. They were a good family, but a small one. Eliza was their only daughter and her mother dead by the time she married. Her father stayed in India until his death in… let me see where is it…. Ah yes until his death shortly following his daughter's That's about the sum of it. There was no other family."

"What about their friends, the people who were stationed out there with them? Was there anyone by the name of George Pearce?"

"There was a Captain by that name, let me see…" he searched through his paperwork.

"Peabody, Pearson, Penwick, ah here we are Pearce. Captain and his wife Margaret. They had one son, George."

"That's him. Who is he?"

"Ah well he I'm afraid he had a very strange life. He was brought up mostly in India so it seems. Eliza and George would definitely have known each other. His mother and father spoiled the boy and he grew up very arrogant, by some accounts. However, there are worse accusations than that…"

Like what?"

"Well I'd rather not say in front of a lady."

"Well I'd rather you just told me."

He huffed and shuffled uncomfortably before lowering his voice and leaning in.

"It's reported he had unnatural habits."

"Do you mean he was homosexual?" Anna said evenly, because if that's what you mean I'd rather you just said it.

His face turned scarlet, and he managed a squeak and a nod.

"Right well that is interesting information," Anna leaned back in her chair.

So George definitely wasn't Eliza's lover, he was simply a great friend. Someone she confided in and vice versa. From George's letters he clearly thought well of her but if he was homosexual, then that would mean the 'affair' she'd been worried about was nothing of the kind.

This was great news.

She smiled at the ferrety man.

Thank you, that is all the information I require."

She stood to leave and he looked at her stunned, his face making a gaping O.

She turned back to him at the door, "What happened to George?"

"I believe he went to America."

Anna nodded and left.

CHAPTER TWENTY-SEVEN

Prisoner

As evening fell, he was restless and keen to move on. But, it was well into darkness when Pierre and he left again, the others also packing up and leaving.

Pierre and he set out on foot and some of the others, also on foot, went in different directions. Someone else took the truck. He didn't question why they weren't in the vehicle but Pierre caught his look back.

"It's safer on foot at the moment," he said

Johnson shrugged, "I trust your judgement."

Pierre said nothing and turned ahead into the darkness.

Johnson caught up with him and kept pace as they trudged over the hills and clusters of trees that hid them from the road.

It was close to dawn when they reached a town.

Pierre obviously knew the place well and took him on a confusing route of alleyways and back secluded streets, before stopping at the back entrance of a house where a young pretty girl with blond hair, took him into a house.

Pierre shook his hand, "I will leave you with Marie. She will take you on the train to your next rendezvous. Good luck."

"Thank you Pierre for all your help."

Pierre nodded and left, disappearing into the morning sunrise.

"Now," said Marie in heavily accented English, "we will leave for the morning train shortly. I have fresh papers for you. But now you change clothes. You look like you sleep in…" she waved her hand disgustedly at his current outfit.

"I did," he said as she handed him a pile of clothes.

A short while later, they marched up the station steps for the first train of the day.

She chatted to him in German, in the open station, some story of her friend being in love with two soldiers and not being able to choose between the two.

She had instructed him not to speak, despite his good German, just in case - unless he had to. So, as she chatted away, probably some made up story, he nodded, and when she asked his opinion he shrugged.

She then started talking about their wedding, apparently they were engaged, or so the story went, so when the train pulled up she was talking about how she would like three bridesmaids and her mother was planning to make strudel, but she was sure her father would come around.

Johnson's heart beat out of his chest as he saw an Army Officer coming towards them. The train had become crowded so the officer had to squeeze past them and Johnson found himself almost cheek to metal with his Iron Cross as the officer excused himself past Johnson and the girl, now chatting about wedding clothes.

He thought it highly amusing that underneath this ordinary German suit he was wearing an RAF crested PT vest and, had the Officer x-ray vision, he would have seen right through to the truth, but as it was the officer moved on up the train and the girl still chattered away.

However, he didn't stop holding his breath until he saw the officer get off at a station further down the line.

As the train moved out of the towns, it emptied enough for them to get a seat and they were left alone as everyone else kept their eyes away from each other. The lull of the train made Johnson feel quite tired and he began fighting the urge to doze off to sleep.

As the train pulled into the station in France some hours later, he kept Marie just in front of him as he followed her down the steps and onto the platform. She headed away from the ticket barrier where the Gendarmes and Secret Police were demanding everyone's papers. She moved towards the station cafe and inside waiting for them was another girl, this time dark haired and petite. The two girls embraced and then indicated that he should follow. They moved towards to toilets at the back and inside a locked door at the back of the room opened up onto the street. The dark haired girl had a key and opening it wide, they stepped out into the busy crowded street unnoticed.

Marie, went one way and the dark haired French girl took him another, down a series of back streets and alleys, to a house, where upon entering she took him upstairs to an attic area with low sloped ceilings and a cold ice chill whistling around the dark empty space.

"How long will I be here?" He asked.

"Just until nightfall, but you must be silent, we have a German officer billeted here, he is right below you, please be silent."

Johnson nodded and laid down to sleep a while on the hard wooden floor.

It was some hours later when the sound of humming woke him, he laid still listening, it was a tune he didn't recognise and was directly below him.

He moved on his belly and peered through the tiny cracks in the floor, he could just make out the outline and colors of a Nazi uniform and he laid still watching, fascinated, as the officer hummed away while removing his Jackboots.

He turned over and stared up at the roof joists above him as he listened to the noises of the house below. It was dark when the girl came to get him, the air filled with chill night and he winced as he sat up, his back aching. He stood as best he could in the small space to stretch it out and release some of the stiffness.

"Come," the girl said an urgency in her whisper.

He did as he was told, being careful not to make a sound on the floorboards as they moved from the attic, down through the house and out of the back door, as silent as the night itself.

She held her finger to her lips and beckoned for him to follow. He did so, and they moved through the town hiding from patrols and anyone searching for those breaking curfew.

They headed away from the station towards the train yard and she pushed him into an empty goods Carriage and followed him in.

"We wait here until morning, then we get on the train that heads towards Treboul near Brittany. There we find a boat and you go to England."

"Thank you,' he said, feeling like he must say something to this girl who was risking her life for him.

She made a French guttural noise in her throat, "I do it not for you English, but for a free France."

He nodded, and sat back to wait, the night seemingly long and endless stretching out before him.

As dawn broke, he rubbed his eyes and face as exhaustion pulled at him, but his mind sharp - acutely aware of every noise and shift in the air. They stepped down from the carriage and the girl looked around her, cautiously moving around the edges of the carriages parked together waiting for action.

They hid, pressing themselves against the side as a worker sauntered by in overalls, shouting greeting at someone they couldn't see.

Once passed, they silently moved out and away, looping through and behind the bushes, coming out at the end of the station platform.

The girl straightened and smoothed her clothes standing purposefully at the edge of the platform, looking expectantly along the track.

Johnson stood beside her, his eyes darting, but they had got away with it.

As the train pulled up and they boarded, they settled for the journey to Treboul, which was long and he found it difficult to stop his mind whirling. He desperately wanted to sleep and the bone tiredness filled his body like lead weights, yet sleep evaded him as he watched and waited, alert to every noise the train made. His heart pounded at every stop, when every patrol entered the train, every time his papers were checked, every time the train moved off again. The temptation to get off and just run for it, to head for cover, to get away from this unsafe observed, public place was almost too tempting to resist, but the girl held his hand firmly, giving him a grounding, giving him something to focus on. He needed to get his head straight, but the broken sleep was making him go mad.

He couldn't wait for it to be over and his bone tiredness only staved off by the thought that he was nearly there.

So much closer now.

It wouldn't be long, just a little further.

How long could he continue to stay lucky? He stubbornly

pushed the thought to the back of his mind.

He was going to succeed.

There was no way he was going back to any damned prison camp.

CHAPTER TWENTY-EIGHT

Anna

Anna couldn't help but keep remembering what one young soldier had said to her the day before. He said there was a fine line between love and hate and no matter how hard she tried, his wise words kept returning, playing over and over in her head like a song repeating.

He had been fairly quiet on the ward and was one person Anna had struggled to engage in conversation, so instead she had tried the tactic of talking of her life in London, which led her onto the doctor saying how much he drove her mad, and his answer to her was to imply it wasn't hatred at all that she felt, but quite the opposite.

She was musing through the library, but only so she could be left to her own thoughts. Still, she wandered feeling a little lost and honestly didn't know what she was doing.

As she left and moved to the main staircase to see what she could do to help, she passed a maid on the stairs going up to the top floor, bucket and cleaning supplies in hand.

"Where are you going?" she asked.

"To clean the room on the top floor."

"Which one?"

"It's on the left?"

"Lord Thomas' room?"

The girl shrugged, "Yes miss."

"I'll do it," Anna said holding out her hand for the bucket and cleaning supplies.

The girl looked surprised but didn't hesitate.

"If you're sure," she said seeming more than a little happy about not having to do the task herself.

Anna nodded and moved towards the top floor, she needed to keep busy or she would go mad.

Even with the bustle of the hospital and helping the patients, it wasn't the same. She missed London, she missed its atmosphere, she missed its people, and for goodness sake she even missed the stink of the place, the smell of brick, plaster, dust, fire and damp.

It had always been home and worst of all she missed having purpose, something to say she was good at. Here she was a spare part, a random estate owner milling around with nothing to do all day. She really didn't like to admit there was probably a million duties she should be taking care of but had no idea what they were because she'd been stubborn about Flynn, with good reason, but nevertheless…

She sighed as she pushed open the door to Thomas' room.

She set the bucket down and rang the cloth in the warm water squeezing it out before tackling the windows and windowsills.

She relished the work and set about giving the place a thorough clean, pleased as each window came up cleaner and brighter as she worked.

Once the windows were done she rubbed her aching arm but feeling much more positive she just needed to be busy.

She set about cleaning the drawers and dusting the surfaces. Then she lifted the heavy rug and put it outside in the hall, she'd take that outside and deal with the cleaning of it.

She then set about cleaning the wooden floor working on her hands and knees making sure she got every inch of the corners.

As she moved towards the middle of the room where the rug had been one of the floorboards moved slightly and lifted at one side when Anna leaned on it.

She stopped, wiping her hands on a dry cloth and made the same movement again with her hands, the floorboard moved again and she caught the edge before it fell snugly back into place. Lifting carefully, the floorboard came away easily and Anna peered inside. There tucked beneath it in the floor cavity was a very dusty envelope.

Anna reached in and retrieved it, sneezing as the dust shifted and got in her nose.

Opening it she reached in and pulled out a small hard book. She gasped to see it. It was a German passport document.

She opened the pages and inside was a picture of her brother, Lord Thomas in a Nazi uniform with a name of Fritz Heinzberg. Her heart pounding she blinked, not believing what she was seeing.

He really was a traitor. Maybe that's why he was killed - our side found out he was a traitor.

Her heart pounding, she reached in and felt something metallic, she withdrew it and silent tears ran down her face as she looked at a Nazi party badge.

She stuffed both items back inside the envelope and stored them back in their hiding place.

She returned the rug to its place and stood outside for a few moments calming her breathing.

There was only one person who might be able to help this situation and she really hated to have to do it but there was really no choice. She had to know.

She remembered the cleaning supplies and retrieved them before heading back downstairs, handing them to a passing maid as she went straight to the telephone.

She called the ferrety man's office and his secretary answered with a whine.

"It's Victoria Leyac, I must be put through directly. She said using her official name. She was learning that it gave her a little more power than her own.

"Miss Leyac," came the ferrety voice.

"I need you to get in touch with Flynn, I need to see him at once."

There was a pause.

"Oh come now, I know you're still in touch with him, stop the pretence and do as I ask. It's vital I see him, tell him it's about Thomas and is really important. More important than anything else."

"I.. ah.. well.. in that case, I will see if I can find him Miss…"

"Just do it will you and hurry."

Anna hung up.

She wasn't sure she'd done the right thing, but then, what was the right thing?

She didn't know anymore, she wasn't sure she ever did know.

All she knew was she needed answers and Flynn was the one who might be able to give them.

CHAPTER TWENTY-NINE

Prisoner

At Treboul, Johnson looked around, the place was a small port and there the girl left him with an man in his middle fifties. He said MI9 had sent him and he had yet another set of fresh clothes and papers for him.

This time he was dressed like a French fisherman and was instructed to meet with a handful of Frenchmen who were trying to get to England to join the war.

These Frenchmen had a plan to hide themselves on a 40 foot fishing vessel until morning and when the vessel left for the early catch, they'd sail along into the open sea.

As darkness fell, the men and Johnson quietly moved down the hill towards where the boat was sat in the mud and waited as they watched the armed German Sentries patrolling the quay. Then as each sentry turned around and moved the other way, one of the men would dash from their hiding place drop down to the harbour floor and then climb on board the boat. It was by far the riskiest thing he'd done and he found his heart pounding as he watched each of the Frenchmen moving along the quay and up onto the boat. When it was his turn he ran out into the cold exposed air and dropped down, the climb up onto the boat seemed to take ages and he was sure that he must be caught, but no, as he reached the top, he found that he had not been seen and the sentry was only just turning round to patrol the other way again. He let out a breath and calmed his breathing to a normal pace. He was almost there; he could smell home. The salt air seemed to breathe England and he lay still, listening to the sentry's footsteps.

When all of the escapers had safely stowed themselves in the bottom of the boat, they waited in silence until the early sunrise glinted through the deck boards above them and the tide lifted the boat off the mud and it bobbed gently. The captain and his crew of two arrived and began making the boat ready to move.

As the boat rattled along, away from the harbour wall and moved painfully, slowly towards the entrance to the harbour, a point where it narrowed between some rocks on the port bow, and with a German guardhouse on the starboard wall.

The boat was required to stop for a final inspection before moving off out to sea, and all below paused, breath held, he felt his heart hammering in his chest as the Captain pulled up, and they hoped the sentries decided not to climb on board to do an in-person inspection, painfully aware that at any moment it could all be over.

Johnson listened to an altercation that seemed to break out at the guardhouse, but as they were speaking French, Johnson didn't understand what was being said.

The Frenchmen next to him laughed silently as the boat chugged into life and they moved off, Johnson breathed a sigh of relief before asking what had been said.

He told him two resistance members had posed as disgruntled citizens and complained to the guards. In the disturbance, they waived us on so they could deal with the complaints.

He smiled, they were good those resistance. Now they were heading out to sea and very soon he'd be home.

The day was painfully slow as they passed German ships and seaplanes, any of which could catch them at an moment.

Finally they made it out into open sea and when night did finally arrive, the heavy winds tossed the boat side to side and Johnson, sitting in the corner, vomited the whole night reminding himself why he had not joined the Navy.

The night was endless as his stomach lurched and heaved, with every movement, the seconds ticking by slowly.

When morning broke, the sea was calmer and he was able to gain some sense of composure and went up to take some breaths of air. The French fishermen thought it a huge joke, how sick he'd been and laughed heartily as they went about their work.

By this point the Frenchmen said they were far enough away from the coast of France to feel safe enough to put out the French Tricolour with the Cross of Lorraine - the sign of the Free French, to show any English patrols they weren't a threat.

The day passed quietly and desperately slowly and as he got closer to home, the more he felt impatient to get there, and the endless waves and rocking motion just seemed to go on and on forever.

As another evening fell, a drizzle set in and he was forced to sit below again, which still smelt distinctly of vomit, despite his bucket having been cleaned up.

He must have slept some because he woke to shouting that they had sighted land.

He rushed up to see for himself and sure enough there was the coast of England in the morning light.

As he watched he saw a small boat approaching, and despite the fact it most likely was friendly, Johnson still felt anxious, having been surrounded by enemies for so long. He was almost there now and nothing was going to stop him.

He was too close to fail.

As the boat approached and the call from it rang out, Johnson smiled broadly as the welcoming sound of a Cornish accent fell on his ears and after so long in foreign lands, he almost wept with relief, although he wasn't about to admit that to anyone.

He cleared his throat and called back. As the boat pulled alongside, A man in a dark suit waved at him,

"Hello, I've been sent to fetch you, Captain, Welcome home. Our Cornish friends here are going to direct your vessel through the minefield and safely to shore, I will meet you there.

He waved back, never so happy in all his life than at that moment, his mind fit to explode, as his body filled with relief and happiness.

As they moved the vessel into dock he stepped off into the cold drizzly English winter, he was handed a hot cup of the best tea he had drank in months and a plate of delicious sandwiches.

While he ate, the man in the dark suit explained that MI9 had sent him and were very keen they set off for London right away.

"I have taken the liberty of allowing you time to bathe and change into uniform, it wouldn't be proper to appear like you are in front of your superiors."

"No sir," he said amused, but he was grateful for the bath and change, he hadn't been able to get one since staying with the nuns, and that had been ages ago he thought, ignoring the thought that he must stink.

"MI9 were keen to get you back as soon as possible once we knew where you were and that you were alive, so some of the arrangements were very roughly organised, but never mind, you're here now. We are to head directly to the Great Central Hotel for debrief."

"A hotel? Where is it?"

"Ah, yes, it's been requisitioned, there's limited space at MI9 HQ, the Metropole, so escaped POW's are debriefed at the Great Central. It's opposite Marylebone station."

"I see."

"So Captain tell me how was your journey? Not too rough I hope."

"If it's all right with you Sir, I'd just like to get changed and have a short rest before getting to London."

"Ah yes, of course, don't let me detain you. Let's save it for the debrief. Ah, and here's a copy of today's paper, I'm sure there's a lot you need to catch up on from this end."

He was guided to and left alone in the room of a guest house, where a bath had been ran for him, a freshly pressed and pristine uniform hung on the outside door of the wardrobe, with socks and shaving implements next to them on the dresser.

He fingered the material looking at the uniform. It would be too big, he decided, but never mind, it was still good to see one looking so new and clean he thought smiling.

He headed to the bathroom and took his time hardly believing he was really back, expecting at any moment a German to come in and march him at gunpoint to the camp.

He scrubbed himself raw, trying to scrub away the lingering stain of captivity and returned to his room once the water had cooled. He began dressing in the fresh uniform feeling he'd never felt anything so crisp and clean next to his skin before, and opened the newspaper on the bed while he buttoned up his shirt.

As he flicked through the pages while tucking the shirt into his trousers, there was one headline that caught his eye,

Great Houses are being Requisitioned for the War.

He stopped tucking his shirt in his trousers again and read, his mind wandering to Olivia, he was dreading this, but it must be done.

Setting his jaw he shut the paper and finished getting ready, he would have to deal with this quickly, there was no sense dragging things out.

CHAPTER THIRTY

Anna

The weather that morning was dark, cold and the air smelt of a brewing storm. Anna woke with aching arms after scrubbing her brother's room the day before.

As she laid there she could feel the cold damp air and pulled the blankets further to her chin.

The wind whistled around the roof and Anna sensed something in the air.

She hadn't heard from Flynn and she felt a kind of silent trepidation at the prospect, but equally knew there was little other choice. She had to know for certain whether the overwhelming evidence pointed where she suspected.

There was the report card, which suggested he had an obsession with Fascism and Mosely, the letter in German and then the photo and party badge.

If he had been a British spy undercover in some way, he surely would have no need to hide German letters, and he wouldn't have Nazi party badges and photos of himself hidden in his room, which, when all was considered, was a damn stupid place to hide sensitive information. He must have been a complete fool, maybe that's why he managed to get himself killed.

Anna sat up with a shiver and yawned. She was damned if she was going to sit here and drive herself mad wondering. She would just have to keep busy and wait to hear from Flynn.

However, she didn't have long to wait, but the time she was ready and onto her third tea of the morning, Flynn had waltzed in, along with a driving rain and icy cold wind.

He looked around at the changes, but his face remained blank and expressionless, ignoring the new hospital receptionist now stationed in the hall, who enquired after his purpose.

"It's okay Phyllis. He's here for me."

The girl nodded and went about her work.

Flynn raised an eyebrow but made no comment.

"We can talk in the green room," she said.

"Ah, so some things are still the same then?"

"Well, no it's the doctor's office now, but we can use it if it's unoccupied, which it should be, as it's time for his morning rounds."

Flynn scoffed but said nothing further.

The green room was empty and there were paper and pencils neatly stacked on the desk.

Flynn took in the room and Anna noticed his eyes linger on everything new and different.

A lonely stethoscope sat on the desk, a white coat flung over the chair, a stained mug on the table. Medical books stacked on the shelves, the photos and ornaments all gone, but most of all he was interested in the large plan of the house and grounds pinned to the wall. He pointed to a section in the back garden area marked in a square near the kitchen garden.

"What is the purpose of this?" he said tapping his finger on the area.

"We're extending the kitchen garden into this adjoining area so the patients can convalesce by doing something useful, practical and that helps the war effort."

"So, you're ripping up all those plants and flowers to grow more veg?" he said tapping the map again.

"Yes."

"Some of those roses have been there since Queen Victoria came to the throne. You can't do that."

"I understand your concern, but this is necessary for the hospital, the men and indeed the war. After all we can't feed them roses."

Flynn sighed, "Well at least tell me you're going to move them to a suitable spot?"

Anna said nothing.

"You're going to let them die?" No, No! This I will not allow. You may destroy this house and everything your brother worked for but this is simply too far." Anna sat silently for a moment.

"What would you suggest?"

"Well, it's possible to move them, but they would need some light and conditions… perhaps here," he said tapping the side of the house on the map.

"Could the patients not tend the flowers and plants as well as the veg, Why do we have to get rid of all the plants?"

"Practically speaking because we can feed them with veg."

"But if they could be moved to a more practical spot, that would mean the continuation of both - is that not a better solution? Plus, there's the idea that growing plants and flowers may help them with their convalescence."

"Perhaps," she said.

"Flynn signed and sat down, "You are abominably frustrating Miss Forrester. Can you not see the useful practical experience I can provide and stop fighting me at every turn. I have knowledge of this place and have devoted my life to it. Can you not accept that I can stop you making some grave amateurish decisions, which will ultimately ruin everything."

Anna prickled but knew he was right. She just didn't like the idea of it and certainly didn't trust his motives.

"Before we get into that there's a matter of extreme sensitivity I wish to put to you. My better judgement says not to trust you, but you are the only one who may have the answers I'm looking for."

Flynn raised an eyebrow.

Anna took a steadying breath.

"Whatever you think of me and regardless of the despicable things you have done, which make me wary of your motives, I do believe you cared for my brother and would protect him. There is something I must disclose to you, but doing so, I put you and myself at great risk. However, I need answers and I think you might be the only one who could give them."

Flynn narrowed his eyes and lit a cigarette before responding, "go on, Miss Forrester," he said sitting back in a chair by the small shelf.

"I suspect my brother was a traitor."

Flynn didn't react and took a drag on his cigarette, the only tell-tale sign of any emotion was a slight frown that creased his forehead.

"On what grounds?" he said evenly.

"A combination of evidence, I found an old school report card that said he was obsessed with Mosely and fascism. I found a hidden letter addressed to him in German behind one of his drawers, then I saw a photo of him with a Nazi soldier hidden under the floorboard with a Nazi party badge.

Flynn sighed and rubbed his forehead, "I know what you're speaking of and I share your concern."

"You knew all this time? Did you report him?"

"No, certainly not."

"Why?"

"Because Miss Forrester, I couldn't bear to, so instead I protected him. I know what the evidence says, but I cannot believe it of the man I knew."

"Even though, withholding evidence makes you treasonous?"

"Yes, even with that I protected him."

"You were in love with him."

Flynn raised his eyebrows in surprise, for a few seconds before recovering himself and masking his feelings again.

"Like I said before, I cared and would do anything to protect him and now his memory - even from himself."

"You must have loved him, to protect him like that and more than a brother or friend. You loved him as a lover."

"We were never lovers, your brother is not... well in any case it seems you have found my Achilles heel, but what are you to do with it, that's the question."

"I don't care about your reasons, I care about why. I asked you here to get your opinion on whether my suspicions are correct.

"I have long wondered the same, although I was never entirely certain. At university Thomas was friendly with a foreign student, Claus, a German, and he got your brother further involved with Mosely's black shirts. He even went over to stay with Claus shortly before the war, but then the war started and he stopped mentioning him, and lost interest in fascism, so I assumed, he had decided that this loyalties remained with his country."

"Did you ever ask him?"

"No, I was tempted, but if I am honest, I was worried about what answer I would get, so decided the best action would be to stay ignorant."

"That doesn't sound like the Flynn I know."

"There's a lot of things you don't know about me."

"Given the evidence now, by rights, we should report our findings to the authorities."

"I don't think that's a good idea," he said.

"Even though concealing it could be considered treasonous?"

"Yes. I've worked very hard over the years to make sure this family and estate is protected, and it's not right to start destroying that when he's gone. He may have been a collaborator, and God knows I hope he wasn't, but he's gone now and can't do any further harm."

"I understand your point of view, but not telling makes us co-conspirators."

"Only if he was alive and it was going on now. It's over and he's gone. There's no sense in bringing up thing that are dead and finished."

"Yes and that was your view of me too - keep it hidden - keep it secret. I'm not sure I can do such a thing. I will not betray my country."

"Oh, you damned infuriating woman, you…"

Whatever Flynn was about to say was lost as the door to the green room banged open and an angry thin man stood there, his blond hair coming free from what would have started as a side parting, he was thinner than the photos she had seen and his uniform hung off him slightly.

CHAPTER THIRTY-ONE

Prisoner

He found it hard to take in the state of London, and couldn't help but compare it to before the war. He just stood and stared at the destruction his mouth agape, the London he knew now a giant wounded animal, calmly carrying on with its daily life despite barely standing.

At the Grand Central hotel, he waited in a converted room, looking out the window at the tube station opposite and the people going about their daily lives, the cold winter air, giving a chill harsh reality to the broken city.

He smoothed an invisible wrinkle in his uniform, and tugged at his collar a little, he desperately wanted to get home.

A large man with a red face, and a Colonel's uniform, entered the room, mopping his brow with a handkerchief as he came in.

"Ah Captain, sit, do sit down," he motioned to a chair. "Now, we are very pleased to have you home, however you must tell us what happened."

He sighed.

"Well sir, I was picked up as planned but we weren't long

into our flight back when the plane was shot and started leaking fuel. The pilot managed to aim the plane at a nearby farm field, but we were still being shot at, and then I'm not sure how it happened, but the pilot hit his head during landing and was dead on impact. The plane was intact but badly damaged. I knew it was vital they didn't find out who I was, so swapped jackets with the pilot, stole his ID and pretended to be him from then on. It was the only way sir, to stop them getting the information I had. The op was at stake, and I had to think quickly."

The officer frowned, "Normally we don't hold with impersonation, however, in this case I think you have acted in the only way possible given the circumstances. Obviously, Johnson's family will have to be told that he is dead, and you will have to return to yours, who will get something of a surprise I think."

"If there had been any other way..."

"I understand, do not worry Captain Leyac, I know MI9 are keen for your information from the op and what went wrong. They need to know where the leak happened, as we've assessed, you must have been compromised. However there is a further matter we must discuss."

"Oh?"

"It seems Captain Leyac that while you have been away, your missing sibling has come forward and claimed your estate. I would, if I were you, return and sort out your affairs. You have been granted a period of leave, following a further debrief and detailed report on all of Victor's information."

"Yes sir, thank you sir. I am aware of this. What's her name, Anna was it?"

"I believe so, Captain. And one more thing..."

"Yes sir."

"Given the increased attention and discussion surrounding your family at present, it is unwise to allow you any further field operations. I know there was some worry over this in the beginning and it was decided the risk was minimal, now however, we believe this is no longer the case and you should cease field operations immediately, for the foreseeable future at least."

"What am I to do?"

"Do not worry Captain, we have plenty of work you can be getting on with, but we will discuss this on your return. Major Carmack will be in to debrief you shortly. Once you have your house in order, you are to report back to Major Carmack. And, we'll need a detailed report of where you were held, weak spots, the guards, that sort of thing.

"Yes sir."

He nodded and stood to leave.

Captain Leyac took the opportunity to pour more tea from the pot in front of him and stood crossing the room to look out the window, thinking.

Major Carmack came in and he turned to greet the large imposing figure he knew well.

"Leyac my boy. Good to have you back. It was a damned rough day when we thought we'd lost you. Now sit and take me through everything."

"As planned Sir, I'd again infiltrated the stationed Army unit and things had been going reasonably until I saw someone I knew from before the war, someone I'd known at school."

"Who?"

"Claus his name was, anyway I convinced him I'd joined the Reich and changed my name because I wanted to be accepted."

"And he believed you?"

"Yes, we'd had some dalliances in our youth with political research, shall we say, so he believed me. Well, I thought he did. I was sure the plan was perfect, but the unit knew there was a leak and so the general started laying traps to catch me. My contact heard chatter they were closing in and I was compromised, so I followed protocol and requested an extraction."

The major nodded, "This we know, we arranged the extraction with one of our most successful cells, so what went wrong?"

"The night Johnson picked me up went smoothly, almost too smoothly, until we were taking off and they were right on our tail, but Johnson was a good pilot and got us up in the air. Fighters followed but we thought we'd lost them in cloud cover, that was when we were hit. Johnson was killed on impact and I had seconds to think, so stole his uniform moved him out of the pilot seat and doused the plane with fuel before setting it alight, it was the only way. If they had known Victor was on that plane, it was safer if they assumed I'd died and the survivor was just the pilot there to fly Victor home."

The Major sat back, "now Captain, the night you found your cover was blown, there was a report due, one we were keen to hear and which you were never able to deliver. Tell me Captain, do you have that information still?

"I do Major."

"Excellent my boy, excellent."

The major sat back and lit a cigarette, picking up the telephone and instructing the person on the other end to put him through. There was a pause before the Major simply said, "It's intact," then paused listening and before replacing the receiver.

CHAPTER THIRTY-TWO

The Final

THOMAS

The closer he'd got to Leyac House, the more he'd convinced himself his legacy had been compromised by some imposter - after all everyone knew his twin was a boy.

What fool would believe the nonsense it was a girl. A brother is what he'd searched for.

Flynn must be a damned fool to believe such rubbish.

He rubbed his temple as he watched the rain stream sideways from the window of the train, as the great beast ploughed its way north.

Could he not trust anyone?

He thought back to the beatings he'd taken at the camp, then further still to his compromised mission. He was lucky to be alive, never mind back home.

The debrief had been very long and he'd spent many hours recounting every detail of his operation, crash, the prison camp and his escape.

He'd given them everything, even that he thought there was a mole in HQ, something the Major had vehemently denied, but a frown had creased his brow all the same.

Now the weight of those secrets were in the hands of those they should. He felt a weight had been lifted and all he wanted to do now was get back home and see what a mess Flynn and this girl had done.

The more he thought of it, the more annoyed he got, so by the time he crunched up the gravel driveway, every change just made him clench his jaw and ball his fists.

He passed a couple of soldiers on crutches, and entered the front door. A young woman smiled.

"Hello, who are you here to visit today?"

"Who the hell are you?"

"I… Phyllis sir,"

"Phyllis, where is the person in charge?"

"Doctor is on his rounds, but…"

"No, Julien Flynn."

"Sorry sir, I don't know a Julien Flynn."

"Anna then?"

"Ah, Miss Anna, she's in the doctor's office with a visitor."

"And the office is…?"

"The little green room upstairs, but you can't…"

He turned and headed up the staircase cutting her off.

"Sir!"

He stopped at the bottom step and turned back to her, "Phyllis, this my damned house. I can go where I like."

Her eyes widened, but not giving her chance to speak, turned to take the stairs two at a time.

The place even smelt like a damned hospital.

He was going to kill bloody Julien for doing this.

Banging open the door to the green room he surveyed the two stunned faces. Flynn's face was white and the girl had big eyes that told exactly what she was thinking and right now it was a mixture of surprise and curiosity.

He met her stare coolly.

"What have you done to my house while I've been gone. How could you let the museum get requisitioned? Did you just think because I was gone, you should just give up?"

"That wasn't him, that was me," the girl said.

"Oh was it? Well, why the hell did you let this imposter take over Julien, have you lost your mind?"

"She's not an imposter Thomas," Flynn said quietly.

"How can you be sure? And why does she only come crawling out the woodwork when I'm supposed to be dead?"

"Thomas I'll explain everything but you need to calm down," Flynn said.

"Actually it's you who needs to explain a few things," Anna said, looking at him with distaste.

ANNA

"Apart from the issue that you're here, and we'll deal with that later - I need to know if you're a bloody traitor?"

"A what?" he said, his fists tight at his side and his face red.

"A bloody Nazi spy? Have you sold your country to the Reich, because if you have, brother or no, you're getting reported."

"And why the hell would you think that, you fool girl? And even if I was it's no business of yours, I don't even believe you're part of this family, you're just an opportunist."

Anna opened her mouth to speak but Flynn interrupted, "Thomas, it's true she is your sister, and I've known all along who she was and where she was."

"You? You knew all this time?"

"I'm sorry Thomas, it was a promise I made to your grandmother, and one I have kept faithfully."

"My grandmother? She knew? Did everyone know except me?"

"Not everyone, I didn't know either," Anna said.

He sat down then and put his head in his hands trying to come to terms with it, and Anna, in spite of herself felt a little pity for him but pushed it aside. She had to know the truth, "I've found things Thomas, in your room, things that suggest you're on the side of the enemy," she said.

"Please tell me it's not true," Flynn said.

He looked up at them both, "of course it's not true, you fools. I work for the government."

"The government? But..."

"Yes. Look I can't tell you anything, but I can say that I'm working on behalf of our government and those things you found are because I suspected a leak at HQ but it's being dealt with now, so there's no need to worry."

Flynn relaxed visibly, but Anna, looked at him still unsure. He noticed. "It's true, I can't say anything more I've signed the Official Secrets Act. I shouldn't even be telling you this. I had to hide some things related to an early mission because of the leak, but they'll be gone within the day."

"But I found an old letter from Mosley saying you were a Blackshirt."

"A blackshirt? Rubbish. And, it wasn't from Mosley, it was from someone I was watching, again only here because of the leak. Obviously that was a mistake when you've got nosey imposters going through your stuff."

Anna didn't react to this and let Flynn step in, "Thomas, I'm sorry I deceived you all these years, but I was faithful to the task I was set and have been thoroughly loyal to you always. I never swayed and never stopped to question it. I did as instructed and believed it was for the best."

"You thought it was best to let me spend my life, my money and my energy looking for a brother you knew all along didn't even exist?"

"I thought you might give up."

He jumped up then, glaring down at Flynn, "You are no friend of mine…"

"Flynn, maybe you should let Thomas and I speak alone for a while and give him chance to calm down, then we can look for a way forward," Anna said.

Surprisingly, Flynn nodded and looked back at Thomas, his eyes sad and for the first time since she'd met him - vulnerable.

He left the room leaving them alone.

"So," Thomas said, "what now?"

"Now I tell you everything, from the beginning. And I have written evidence and proof, and there's a letter for you from our mother, a diary and some other things you might want to see, but first I need to explain."

The two of them sat for hours and Anna told him everything, from the beginning, her own story, how she found out, their parents, everything and he listened patiently and quietly while she spoke.

When she had finished, he stood and looked out the small window his back to her.

"It's a lot to think about," he said to the window.

"Come," she said, "I have something to show you."

THOMAS

He stared up at the elfin-like face and big eyes and felt like he needed to reach out and touch it.

Was it real?

Was this whole thing real?

He looked over at Anna, and noticed a small resemblance to the elfin face portrait of Lady Eliza, now right in the middle of his gallery.

"Let's walk in the gardens Anna, we have much to talk about,"

She followed him outside and the two of them walked towards the family graves.

"So tell me," she said, "why were you reported dead at all if you weren't,"

"Well I had to do it that way, everyone had to believe I was gone so the Nazi's didn't find out."

"Why? Where have you been?"

"I've been in a POW camp, but escaped, with the help of some nuns, a crazy Frenchman and a few others."

"So were you and Johnson together then? Did he escape too?"

"How do you know about… Oh wait, Olivia."

Anna nodded.

"That's the difficult part, I was the only one who escaped that place crash, I pretended to be Johnson. He died that night."

Anna stopped then, her face going white, "Olivia. She's been writing to him all this time."

"Yes that was me."

"You?"

"It's not going to be easy telling her."

"She's here."

He stopped then and looked at her, his heart pounding, "she still here? Where?"

"She's the hospital ward Sister."

"Go, go speak to her, we have time to catch up,"

He turned and sprinted back towards the house but paused hearing Anna call him back, "it's good to have you back," she said smiling.

He found Olivia, just coming out of the dining room, which was now a ward and recognised her instantly.

"Olivia."

She looked up curiously, "Can I help?"

"I need to speak to you, take a walk with me."

"I'm sorry, sir I'm busy."

"I'm Thomas Leyac."

"You are? But I thought you were dead. Oh Anna will be so pleased, where is she…"

"Olivia, it's important I speak to you. Walk with me in the garden."

She followed him outside and they strolled along the rows of plants.

"There's no easy way to tell you this, so I'm going to just say it. Johnson is gone, he died the night of the plane crash. I was the one in the plane with him and because of my work I had to pretend I was him…."

"Don't say that, why would you say that. I've been getting letters."

"It's true Olivia, those letters are from me, I was the one writing to you. It's me you've been writing to."

"That's a horrible thing to do. Why would you?"

"I had no choice, I'm so sorry Olivia."

She turned to walk away from him but he touched her arm to stop. "Please Olivia, I need to tell you…"

"Tell me what, that you're a horrid person who makes people believe things that aren't true. That you've been laughing at me."

"No, that I love you. I didn't intend it and it wasn't part of the plan, but I couldn't help myself. I fell in love with you through your words and now I want the chance to get to know you, as myself."

She just stared at him, so he took both her hands and kissed her.

She didn't resist and as he pulled away, he saw tears forming, so hugged her tight.

"I just don't know what to feel now," she said.

"I know, I'm sorry," he said.

She didn't reply.

"Come on we'll go inside and have some tea," he said pulling away and holding out his hand to her.

She hesitated for a moment looking at him, then took his hand in hers.

ANNA

Anna spent a little longer walking the gardens alone, thinking about Thomas and his sudden appearance. Then there was Olivia, she really hoped the loss of Johnson didn't upset her too much, after the blow she'd had in London. Anna was worried how she would cope, and being around Thomas, who, as it turned out, had been writing to Olivia all along. It's not the best situation.

She was so deep in thought, she didn't hear anyone approach and turned when she heard the crunch of footsteps on gravel right behind her.

"Oh Doctor Laker, what are you doing out here?"

"I came to tell you it's time for me to return."

"Have you heard the news?" she said ignoring him.

"Yes I've just seen him with Olivia. How are you doing Anna?"

"I'm fine," she said turning her back on him and walking on.

He rushed to catch her and turned her around, holding her in place, "Still lying to me?" he said concern on his face.

Anna was painfully aware of the touch of his hands and found it hard to speak, "it's a lot to process," she said eventually turning and walking away.

"I have to go back to Abbeyfleam Anna."

"I know."

Silence.

"But I'm worried about you."

Anna laughed, "What's to worry about my brother is

back."

No answer.

"Look Doctor it's all okay, Thomas and I have spoken, we've sorted everything out. You've been great helping out I am grateful, but you must return and take up your responsibilities."

"Well if that's how you feel, good bye Anna."

"Good bye doctor," she said not looking at him.

She heard him walk away.

It was some hours later when she returned to the house, extremely cold but she didn't mind that. She suddenly felt numb inside and couldn't understand why.

She floated through the evening, distracted, her mind not on anything Thomas or Olivia were saying and she went to bed that night feeling restless.

It was early when she woke to a gnawing, empty feeling, and silence all through the house.

In her sleepy, fuzzy state the conversation she'd had with the patient played on her mind, *'you don't hate him at all…'* he had said.

She sat up, her mind suddenly clear.

She had let him go.

And, in the darkness and the cold, at four in the morning, she knew then, knew she'd been foolish.

She'd ran away from all her problems and thought that by working hard to make things stay the way they were, it would somehow stop the changes; somehow stop the loss and grief. That somehow it would stop the mixed-up feelings she had about her mother, her life, the Leyacs, her brother, Flynn, her career, the Doctor…

The Doctor.

She had let him go.

He had been right all along and she knew then, with clarity, she'd been blind. She had let her feelings take over and allowed everything to become a confusion of pain and grief. She hadn't even stopped for a minute to think; really think.

I have to go.

She got up then and got dressed, slipping out the house in the early morning to be at the station as soon as possible.

It had rained again, just as it had the night she lost her mother, but this time, the rain had been brief, but still enough to make the ground muddy. She tramped through the mud down to the village, and waited on the station platform.

The cold made her shiver but she welcomed it; welcomed the pain of the cold in her joints; welcomed the loss of stupidity; welcomed the loss of hesitation.

When the train pulled up, she applied the last of her auxiliary red lipstick, got on without a backwards thought, and smiled as it moved off - taking her to put things right.

To Abbeyfleam.

To him.

Want to be an Early Bird?

Want to read the next book by Sara Thomson?

Then join my exclusive readers club to **find out when the next book is being released.**

Only priority Early Bird Club members get access to the following:

1. The chance to win **free signed copies** of my books
2. Access to **exclusive early bird competitions**
3. Priority access to **upcoming release dates**
4. The opportunity to **help with the writing process** and shape the next story
5. The chance to **have your say** on story ideas and how your favourite characters develop
6. **Advance warning** of events, signings and readings

So don't be shy, **get on board and join the early bird club today** and it could be you getting a free signed copy or an advanced reader copy prior to release.

All you need to do is type the following webpage in your browser to sign up:

https://sarathomsonauthor.co.uk

About the Author

About the Author

From being a very young child reading and writing were a huge part of my life and my mother encouraged this through her own love of books. The very first book I ever wrote was a children's story for my younger sister when I was seven. I painstakingly drew (very badly) little hedgehogs and animals and loved creating the story for her to read. I stuck the book together with sellotape and presented my work to a delighted little girl.

Alongside things like this, I kept a diary throughout my childhood and teenage years, and had so many different stories floating around my imagination that sometimes I just had to write them down to get them out of my head.

However, I resisted this urge to write and kept it a secret, because real people didn't become writers, real people got jobs in offices. But I always told myself I would write a book one day.

Now finally that book is written, alongside a few more, and I've found what I was meant to do. So if you are like me and have always told yourself you would write 'one day', make that one day today. Don't waste time.

Through taking that plunge and deciding to write, I found that it's a passion that doesn't go away with just one book, instead, like a demon inside it wants more books and more stories come raging up begging to be written.

Other than writing, I spent 22 years as a military wife and moved around a lot, gained a BA Hons degree in English with Creative Writing and a Masters degree in Creative Writing, brought up four children and built a career as a Marketing content and copywriter.

For the future, I plan to write and publish more books and help other authors with their writing via my marketing company services https://STWriter.com

If you would like to connect with me on a personal level, to ask questions or for any reason at all, **email me at sara@sarathomsonauthor.co.uk** I always reply to all my reader emails personally.

Printed in Poland
by Amazon Fulfillment
Poland Sp. z o.o., Wrocław

64017289R00150